Maggie
and the Stone Egg

Geraldine Aldridge

For my family...

Illustrated by Peter Milton Holdway
Edited by Frankie Bailey
Editorial Assistant Colin E Aldridge

The Legend

When the ancient Stone Egg cannot glow
For all the words that fill the air
Then comes a maid who you will know
By silvery moonlight in her hair.

By the months of reddish shades
By the bells that cannot ring
By the flowers that will not fade
She shall sing as blackbirds sing.

From careful gardener and from rose
From ancient greenwood she descends.
The Stone Egg with her always goes
Or else the hatching simply ends.

Deep in the Dragon Speakers cave
There waits a rainbow she will meet.
Then Seven Others she must save
So magic cycles may complete.

If such a one as she
Is not quickly found
Then mighty seas will freeze
And darkness shroud the ground

Chapter 1

Egg Keepers and Expectations

Full Moon. May Day.

A team of Morris dancers had taken their places on the road. Their dark hats and socks were trimmed with rainbow coloured ribbons. The small girl thought they looked like crazy black crows as their dark frockcoats flapped in the breeze. The crowd watched. The air smelled of fried onions, candy-floss and popcorn. Bubbles floated in the gentle air and a cloud of cherry blossom petals fluttered down from a tree in the cathedral garden onto the dancers in the street below.

"A dragon, Mum, look!" shouted the girl, tugging on her mother's sleeve as she jumped up and down and pointed at the shape that flapped towards the cathedral spire.

"Yes, darling, some of the Morris dancers are pretending to be a big dragon. He's quite scary isn't he? He's going to fight a battle with St George, look!"

"This dance we are about to perform," announced one of the Morris men, glaring at the eager crowd from beneath his bushy eyebrows, "is from the Dark Side!"

"No, not the one that St George is going to fight!" cried the small girl, "That's just pretend. This is a *real* dragon – look!"

"It's only one of those helium balloons, darling," said her mother, glancing up at the cathedral from the busy street where the brightly dressed Morris dancers and musicians were busy performing the battle. "It's going to get caught up on the ledge. Would you like me to buy you one?"

The sun was shining behind the cathedral spire. The girl screwed up her eyes as the small golden dragon landed on the stone ledge just below the cathedral roof, from where carved grey gargoyles grimaced down at the crowded streets. The little dragon clung fast to the ledge, struggling to get its balance. It seemed to be watching her. She stared at it as it gradually became motionless, its golden shades fading. In a few short minutes it had become the same drab colour as the gargoyles. It seemed to the small girl as if the dragon felt it had to hide.

"Mummy, the dragon is disappearing!" said the small girl.

"Is it, darling?" said her mother vaguely. "Then the battle must be over. Let's go home."

*****

Full Moon. A month earlier.

Maggie threw another handful of peanuts onto the grass for the jackdaws that pecked busily around her feet. Mike was trying to carve his initials into the old stone wall with his penknife. Autumn - Maggie's dog - stretched, stood up and then growled at the jackdaws, rushing at them to chase them away. The birds all flew up to perch on the crumbling castle walls.

"Oh Autumn!" said Maggie crossly. "Lie down you naughty girl!"

Maggie looked up at the jackdaws. The birds were all staring back at her. They seemed to be everywhere - on top of the turrets, in empty arrow-slit windows, in holes in walls where time had stolen a stone or two.

"Look," whispered Maggie. "They're all watching us."

"That is a bit weird," said Mike.

From the top of the castle, a lone jackdaw flapped up into the air and then soared down to land on the grass in front of them. It made a strange downward movement with one wing, gave a sort of trembling twitch and, in an instant, standing on the ground at their feet was not a bird at all but a tiny man. He held a shiny, black feathered bird-cloak in one out-stretched hand. The little man swept them a graceful bow.

"At last," he rasped, "We have found you!"

Maggie and Mike stared at the little man in front of them. He had a sharp chin, pointed ears, and delicate wings like those leftover leaf-skeletons you sometimes find in the winter woods. He was wearing clothes of black silk, a close-fitting grey hood, and shiny, black boots shaped like birds feet.

"You're not a jackdaw at all," Maggie whispered and then blushed red, worried that she might have offended him.

The little man laughed.

"No!" he said, in his strange, rasping voice, "I am one of the Egg Keepers. We wear the birds' plumage so that we may move unnoticed in the world of humans."

He turned and, raising his arm, signaled for the other jackdaws to join him. In a rush and swish of wings there stood before them a crowd, not of jackdaws, but of many tiny men and women. Just as the little man had done, they all swept Maggie and Mike a low and gracious bow.

"We have been waiting for you, Maid Maggie," the little man said, "We believe you are the person of whom Our Legend speaks."

"What legend?" asked Maggie, wondering how on earth he knew her name. But she thought it might be too rude to ask.

"First let me introduce myself," said the little man. "My name is *Chark*."

"Pleased to meet you, *Chark*," said Maggie. "This is my cousin, Mike."

Chark nodded gravely, "Good, good, your cousin Mike," he said. "Now, you must listen very carefully indeed, Maid Maggie and Mike. I have a strange tale to tell you - a tale that starts millions of years ago at the very dawn of time."

"We've got to be home for tea by five," said Maggie.

"Don't worry," said *Chark*. "I will only tell you what you need to know for now. I will begin with Our Legend. It was given to us many centuries ago by one who was very like you, Maid Maggie. And now the time has come for you to explain what it means."

"Me tell *you*?" said Maggie. "How am *I* supposed to know what it means?!"

"We will tell you about Our Legend first," said *Chark*, "and then maybe you will understand a little better."

Maggie stared at Mike and Mike stared at Maggie. Then all the jackdaw people turned their heads towards them and began to chant:

When the ancient Stone Egg cannot glow
For all the words that fill the air
Then comes a maid who you will know
By silvery moonlight in her hair.

Chark paused and nodded at Maggie. He seemed to be waiting for her to speak.

"I really don't know what the first bit means, but that last bit could definitely be about my hair," said Maggie, "because it is sort of silvery. My Nanny Gardner calls it Moon-Blonde."

Mike sniggered a bit and Maggie shot him an angry look.

Chark nodded wisely. "Let us continue," he said to the jackdaw crowd.

By the months of reddish shades
By the bells that cannot ring
By the flowers that will not fade,
She shall sing as blackbirds sing.

Chark was, again, looking at Maggie. She felt it was only polite to try and help him out.

"Well, I suppose that bit about the blackbirds could be me playing my penny whistle in the garden this morning," said Maggie. "I was trying to make blackbird noises to sound like their songs but it didn't really come out very well."

"And the flowers could be those bluebells you stuck in your sunhat," Mike said. He was feeling a bit left out and was happy to see that the little man was smiling at him and seemed pleased with his answer. "But they've gone all droopy already," Mike added, "They won't last much longer."

Maggie looked down at the bluebells she had picked and then tucked inside the band on her daisy-patterned hat. She liked to do word puzzles and this situation was a bit like that. Then she thought of something amazing! "Well perhaps my bluebells are the bells that cannot ring! And maybe it's the *daisies* printed on my sunhat that are the flowers that will not fade!" She was beginning to enjoy herself. Even if she was wrong, this was still a great game!

"So how about the months with radishes then if you're so clever?" said Mike.

"Reddish!" Maggie giggled, "Not radish!"

"Woof!" barked Autumn.

"Oh, you clever dog!" laughed Maggie. "That must mean Autumn! Of course! Her fur is full of different kinds of reddish brown, just like the leaves on the trees that time of year!" And she leaned down to stroke Autumn's glorious chestnut ears.

Chark nodded slowly and cleared his throat. He narrowed his eyes, raised his bony arm up and pointed his skinny finger in the air. The throng of Egg Keepers began their chanting again:

From careful gardener and from rose
From ancient greenwood she descends.
The Stone Egg with her always goes
Or else the hatching simply ends.

"Do you ever walk through the woods to get here, Mags?" asked Mike, sensibly.

"No," Maggie said, "And don't call me Mags. Anyway, there aren't any roses up here. Or gardeners. I can't believe I'm in a legend! Isn't it amazing?!"

"Yeah…" said Mike, feeling just a little bit jealous. He turned and stared at the little man. "How did you know her name?" he demanded. "How did you know my cousin was called Maggie Gardner?"

"We heard you calling her Maggie when we were perched up in the trees. Did you say her other name is

Gardener?" asked *Chark*, his beady little eyes widening.

"Oh," gasped Maggie. "That must be it! But it's Gardner actually! That's spelled a bit different you know!

"*Sounds* the same though, genius," muttered Mike under his breath.

"And my Mum's name is Rose!" Maggie could see more bits of the puzzle gradually beginning to fit together. "And her name was Greenwood, before she married my Dad!"

"So was mine," said Mike, not wanting to be left out.

"Our mums are twins you see," explained Maggie to *Chark*. "Rose and Lily. So could that explain things?"

"Yes," nodded *Chark*. "Yes, indeed, my children. It is all good news. Exceedingly good news!"

"What's exceedingly mean?" whispered Mike to Maggie. But she had this silly dreamy look on her face now and so he gave up waiting for an answer. *Chark* began to chant again and all the other Egg Keepers joined in:

Deep in the Dragon Speakers cave
There waits a rainbow she will meet.
Then Seven Others she must save
So magic cycles may complete.

If such a one as she
Is not quickly found
The mighty seas will freeze.
And darkness shroud the ground

"Dragons!" said Mike. "Fantastic!"

"But the world's going to die!" cried Maggie. "That's awful!"

11

"*Dragons*, Mags!" shouted Mike, getting just a bit over-excited. "There's a dragon's cave with a rainbow in it! Great!"

"Not that great," said Maggie, "It says I've got to save The Seven Others whoever they are. Anyway, how can you get a rainbow in a cave?"

"I think it sounds *well* cool!" said Mike. "If she doesn't want to save them, Mister Birdman, *I'll* do it!"

"He's not asking *you!*" snapped Maggie. Mike really was being a bit of a pain.

Chark and the other tiny people had stopped chanting. They all seemed to be staring straight at Maggie.

"You must understand, Maid Maggie," said *Chark*. He sounded extremely serious, "We are sure it is *you* that we need to save the world. But it is true that many difficult tasks lie ahead of you."

"Look, I'm not agreeing to anything yet, understand?" said Maggie.

"Yeah," agreed Mike, "she can't run off and find some caves just because you say so!"

"I need to be really sure that I'm the person you think I am before I agree to anything!" said Maggie.

Chark smiled at Maggie. At least it looked a bit like a smile. She could not be sure.

"We knew it *might* be you because of your hair which shines like moonbeams in the sun and the sweet way you play your penny whistle in your garden," he explained, "but it was when you called your dog that we were certain. And now you must finally see that Our Legend fits you exactly. We have found you at last and hope you will be able to guide us and allow everything to be alright again."

"But what about all this stuff about shrouds, and stone eggs, and the world dying?" asked Maggie. "It sounds really *horrible!*"

"Yes. The Stone Egg is indeed dying," said *Chark* gravely, "and we don't know why. And if the Stone Egg dies, the dragons will leave. Then the world will freeze and all life on Earth will cease."

"But *what* Stone Egg?!" shouted Maggie. She was beginning to feel very worried and now wished it was Mike who had been chosen instead of her.

"Dragons, Maggie," hissed Mike again, in the hope of encouraging her. "How cool is that?!"

"The dragons are the mountains that curl around the Earth and keep her warm," said *Chark*.

"Are you are saying that mountains are actually *dragons*?" exclaimed Mike. "You honestly can't expect us to believe that! You're having a laugh!"

"I am telling you the whole truth, son of a Greenwood Twin," replied *Chark*. He was looking very offended and the other jackdaw people had started to murmur amongst themselves, "It is up to you what you believe."

Mike felt a little chill run down his spine. But it was not fear. It was excitement. This whole thing was nuts, but his life, he reckoned, had been pretty boring up until today. What's more, he really liked being called the son of a Greenwood Twin. It made him feel important.

"Well, thank you very much, but no thanks!" said Maggie to *Chark*. "If it's all the same to you, I'm going home now with Mike. I'm really very sorry, but if you're looking for a person to go and deal with dragons or mountains or whatever they're supposed to be, I'd rather you found somebody else. I'm getting a headache! Come on Mike!" And she picked up her rucksack. Then, holding firmly on to Autumn's lead, she set off down the hill.

"Maggie!" called Mike, running after her and grabbing at her arm. But Maggie shook him off and carried on walking.

"Come on, Mags…" he said as he drew alongside her, "…don't go! It sounds quite good, I reckon. If Mister Birdman is telling the truth, we might actually get to have an adventure for once!"

"I don't care about adventures!" snapped Maggie, "It's mean of them, trying to pretend that I'm a special person in some silly old legend they've probably just made up! And *don't* call me Mags!" she added.

"Okay, well, if you don't want to do it, I will," said Mike, "I'll do it all on my own! I'm not scared of some rainbow in some cave and a stupid stone egg!"

Maggie stopped hurrying along and turned to face him. "I think you *should* be scared. Anyway, they're not asking you. They're asking *me*."

Mike looked at his cousin and saw that she was deadly serious, "Maybe they'll let me come along and protect you," he said kindly, "Our Mums are Greenwood Twins remember? We're cousins. We're family. Come back up the hill Maggie. Go on. Come back up the hill and let's try and help the bird people!"

Maggie sat down on one of the ruined walls and put her head in her hands. She needed to think. Autumn jumped up to put her paws on Maggie's lap. The dog whimpered and Maggie ruffled the deep, soft burnished fur sticking out from her collar. "We don't believe in silly bird fairies do we, Autumn?" she whispered. A tear trickled down her cheek and she felt terribly sad all of a sudden.

"Birds that turn into people aren't fairies," said Mike. "They're Egg Keepers, remember, not fairies."

Autumn turned her head and looked back up the hill. She was wagging her tail.

"See?" said Mike. "Even Autumn wants us to go back and help them! *She's* not scared!" He sat down on the wall beside his cousin.

14

"But what about the Stone Egg?" Maggie continued. "Whose egg is it? And why is it dying? And why will the world freeze? I just don't get it!"

There was a sudden flurry of fluttering wings behind them. *Chark* landed on the end of the wall. Smoothing his bird-feather cloak, he sidled around to face them.

"I could answer all of your questions children," he said, "if you would only allow me to."

"Well, alright then…" Maggie sighed. "We'll listen for a little bit longer. But it doesn't mean we're agreeing to anything, right?"

Chark leaned forward and lowered his voice, "The Stone Egg is *very* special," he said. "It is not meant to hatch but to rise into the air. If it does not rise up, the dragons have no call to answer. They cannot lay their eggs. They will become unhappy and leave. Then the Earth will grow cold and sad and lonely without the dragons to keep her warm. The land will crack open when the seas freeze over. It will be an end to all living things."

"But how do you *know* this?" Maggie asked.

"Because it has happened before," answered *Chark*.

"Well, life on Earth didn't end *then*, did it?" said Maggie, folding her arms.

"Yeah, we're all still here looking at each other!" agreed Mike.

"It did end," murmured *Chark*. "It ended many millions of years ago. The world had to grow itself all over again out of dust and rock. We call it The Renewal."

"So let it grow back *again* then!" exclaimed Maggie. "It managed it before!"

"But we always need *help* for The Renewal, said *Chark*. We always need the help of a very special human being to start it off - and you, Maggie Gardner, are the one."

"I tell you what, said Maggie. "This is the deal. If you can show me the Stone Egg. Prove to me that it's real. Then I might consider helping you out."

Mike grinned at her. This was a great idea. This might mean Maggie was willing to be persuaded.

Chark pulled his bird-feather cloak close around him. The breeze had turned very chilly. "Very well," he said. "Come back to the hill tomorrow and I will show you the Stone Egg".

"It's going to have to be *very* early in the morning," said Maggie, "Mike and his little sister, Emma, are staying at my house. I'll need to be back there by 7am to help Mum get breakfast for everyone."

Mike pulled a face. Kid sisters could be such a pain. He wondered how he was going to keep this a secret from Emma. She was so nosey. "I know!" he yelled, "We can tell your Mum we decided to walk Autumn early because we wanted to see the sunrise! Tell her we're taking some pictures for a school science project!" He looked very pleased with this brainwave and Maggie had to admit it was a great idea.

"We will be here, waiting for you," said *Chark*.

*****

In his lonely castle on the dark side of the moon sat an old, white dragon. He gazed out of the window at the velvety black sky with its billions of silver stars. The stars stared back at him. The dragon sighed and turned to his desk. He opened the huge book that lay in front of him and flexed his claws. Dipping his longest, sharpest claw into a pot of black ink on his desk he began to scratch some letters onto the white parchment in front of him. And he wrote…

In the Beginning

The Stone Egg hung alone and cold in space.
Wishing to grow, it cried out..
Mournful, lonely words it spoke.

Though faint, so faint, its call was heard.
Light years away a rainbow touched the
ground.
Upon its back many coloured crystal eggs
hatched out..
Baby dragons stretched their legs and wings.
Flying with joy towards the sound,
They landed on the Stone Egg's shell.
The Stone Egg, startled, sensed that all was
well.
They curled their wings around its oval shape.
At last the Stone Egg, sighing, knew that it
was safe.

The white dragon finished writing, and wiped the ink from his claw onto a piece of black rag. He blew on the ink to dry it and sat for a while, reading what he had written. In a voice that creaked like a rusty hinge he announced, "Alone and cold in space!" He gave a huge sigh, closed the book and heaved himself up. He carried the book to a shelf on the wall, disturbing a cloud of white dust which rose like mist around him. He shuffled to the window to gaze once again at the stars. Words rasped in his throat once more. "I'd really love to see a rainbow!" he said. His voice drifted away like bonfire-smoke.

*****

18

Wednesday.

Maggie stood peering out of her bedroom window, waiting for Mike to wake up. Mike and Emma were stopping over for a few days because their Mum and Dad were going away on a special trip. Something to do with their work. *How could the Egg Keepers exist without anyone knowing? They looked just like jackdaws before they took off those cloaks. How could any of it be real?* she thought to herself.

The door hinges creaked and Mike's face appeared. He stepped quietly (for Mike) through the shadow cast by the door and safely into her room. *He loves this,* thought Maggie, noticing Mike's black T–shirt and jeans. *He thinks he's on an S.A.S. mission.* But she was secretly pleased her cousins were staying. Their Mums and Dads often took turns exchanging sleepovers for all the children. It was really good fun. A bit like having two houses really.

At the sight of Mike, Autumn started bouncing around happily.

"Ssssh, Autumn…" whispered Maggie, "…you'll wake Emma up. Got your phone, Mike?' Mike was allowed a phone with a camera. She wasn't old enough to have one yet, her Mum had said.

They walked in silence, Autumn bounding on slightly ahead. It was 5.30am in the morning and the quiet blue sky was beautiful, still flushed with pink and yellow and orange from the sunrise. Mike stopped to take a few shots just in case someone asked to see them. It wasn't *really* a fib about the school project. There was always some science project or other going on. When they had walked a little way along the road, Maggie felt the need to speak, "I was terrified Mum would say no.

19

But the deal is that we must be back by 7am at the latest, okay Mike?"

"I thought the twins would wake up and spoil it," said Mike, "I tried to be ever so quiet. Did you know they snore? It's going to be a nightmare in your house when your Mum has the new baby. It's bad enough for me having Emma as a kid sister but you're stuck with Sid and Colin. Plus a new baby screaming its head off. It's going to be murder!"

"Emma's very sweet and mostly quiet," said Maggie. "You're lucky. Sid and Colin can be so noisy sometimes. And at least the new baby's going to be a girl. Should balance things out a bit."

Mike glanced at Maggie. She was smiling. She did not seem scared at all. He sighed with relief. *It's going to be okay,*" he said to himself.

"I feel like a contestant on one of those TV game-shows," laughed Maggie, "One where you find that before they actually give you the main prize they are going to make you eat a whole bucket of worms!"

"Yeah!" agreed Mike, "Yuk!"

"Whatever it is, bring it on!" declared Maggie, "I'm ready for anything today!"

They had reached the hill beyond the park.

"It's lucky it's still so early," whispered Maggie. "They don't have so many castle guards on duty before opening hours."

The castle which, during the day, was usually busy with sightseers felt a bit spooky despite the pretty sunrise. It crouched like a huge grey monster clinging to the craggy hillside. The shrubs and bushes, too, had a menacing quality as if they hid within their branches all sorts of dangerous creatures that might be watching the children as they walked past.

Maggie and Mike were very relieved to find *Chark* and the other Egg Keepers waiting for them on the old stone wall.

"Here we are, then," said Maggie to *Chark*. "But we've only come to look at the Stone Egg, remember, and we've got to be home by 7am!"

"I understand," said *Chark*. "Follow us, please."

Chark and the rest of the Egg Keepers spread their wings and flew down the daffodil-covered bank and into a gap behind a hawthorn bush. The children followed them. Beyond the hawthorn bush was an opening in the grassy hillside. It was the entrance to a tunnel. The Egg Keepers flew through it and the two children and Autumn crept in behind them.

The ground sloped sharply downwards. The slimy walls gave off a dim greenish glow. There was just enough light to see where they were going. They edged down the tunnel with the Egg Keepers flying ahead, leading the way. Eventually, the tunnel opened out into a huge cave. The children stood still and looked around them. The cave was roughly oval in shape. Watery liquid dripped down from overhead and formed dark pools on the floor. Around the sides, huge stalactites hung dangling from the ceiling and glistening stalagmites rose up to try and meet them, joining with them in places, knitting together with thick strands of greenish slime.

Mike knew all about stalactites and stalagmites from school. "That's funny," he said out loud, "I didn't somehow expect to find a porous chalk cave like this under the castle, did you Maggie?"

"No good asking me," said Maggie dismissively. Porous, indeed! He could be such a show off sometimes.

"I'd have thought you'd know everything," said Mike sarcastically, "seeing as how you're the one chosen by The Legend."

The dripping walls of the cave seemed to creak a little. It felt terribly cold down there. Autumn was panting now, her tongue hanging out. Maggie rested her hand on the dog's head to comfort her. She was starting to feel quite nervous herself.

"It'll be alright," Mike said, but his voice didn't sound very steady all of a sudden.

The Egg Keepers flew over to a large flat rock in the middle of the cave and settled on it. Then the children saw that there was something resting on the rock - an interesting shape hidden in a slight hollow. They walked over to it and gazed down.

"The Stone Egg," announced *Chark*.

*****

"Space…" said the old white dragon to himself, "…really is a very lonely place." He pulled himself slowly up the spiral staircase until he reached the top of the turret. He stood on the platform for some time, gazing at the endless dome of space above his head. It was the dark side of the moon. Then he turned and trudged back down, his long white tail slithering behind him until he was back in his familiar room. He folded himself into his chair, resting his head on the carved stone back-rest.

"A very lonely place is space!" he repeated and, leaning forward, put his head in his hands and sighed deeply.

*****

The cave smelt horribly damp. A strand of green slime dripped from a fang-like stalactite high in the roof and landed with a plop on Maggie's shoulder. She flinched. Autumn whined and pressed against her leg. Maggie and Mike couldn't take their eyes off the egg. It was not very big, about the size of a grapefruit. It seemed to be made of rock of a light brown colour and had tiny cracks all over its rough surface. From within the egg came a very faint glow of golden light.

"Is it alive?" whispered Maggie.

"Only just," said *Chark*, caressing the egg with his tiny hand. "If it stays in this cave it will certainly die." And a tear fell from his wrinkled cheek and landed on the egg. The light within the Stone Egg flickered as he touched it, illuminating *Chark* and his companions and casting shimmering shadows from their wings onto the wet walls. Maggie's eyes started to sting and she was afraid she was going to cry. She felt so sorry for the little people.

"What's inside it?" asked Mike. "What laid it?"

"The Earth laid it," said *Chark*. "Every ten thousand years the Earth lays a Stone Egg like this one, with molten lava at its heart."

"It's beautiful," said Maggie.

"Please…please take it with you, Maggie Gardner," said *Chark*, staring at her intensely.

"But I don't want to," said Maggie, panicking a bit, "I'll mess it up. What would I *do* with it?"

"Go on, Mags," said Mike. "Don't be such a girl!"

Just because I don't climb every tree I pass, thought Maggie, *or jump onto every wall, he thinks I am a coward. For him this is a great adventure. Oh, I really do hate caves!*

She sighed. "Alright," she said. "But you remember this. If it dies, it won't be my fault."

"We entrust it to you," said *Chark*. "Guard it well."

Maggie picked up the Stone Egg carefully. Its shell felt cold and rough in her hands.

Chark and his companions flew to the mouth of the cave, beckoning them all to follow.

The two children blinked as they stepped out into the sunshine. Loud rock music blared out suddenly and Maggie nearly dropped the egg. It was Mike's mobile ringtone. He grabbed the phone out of his pocket: "Hi Aunty Rose!" It was Maggie's Mum. "I'm really sorry…yeah…we're still walking Autumn round the castle…yeah, we'll run home right now." He put the phone back in his pocket.

"Your Mum's really angry, Maggie," he said. "It's already gone 7am!"

The light inside the Stone Egg flickered and vanished.

"I think the egg just died," whispered Maggie. But then it flared once more and she felt a warm tingling in her fingers. "Oh…" she gasped.

"You may still save it," said *Chark*. "There is a little time left."

"I'll try," said Maggie, "but I don't really know how. You'll have to promise to tell me what to do." She tucked the Stone Egg into her rucksack. "What's it going to hatch into?" she asked. "It won't hatch out in my bag will it?"

"It isn't going to hatch," said *Chark*. "I'll explain later when we see you again. We still have much to tell you."

"Maggie, we're in big trouble. We have to run!" urged Mike, tugging on Maggie's sleeve.

A flash-light scanned the grassy bank, making them all jump.

"Oi! What are you kids doing up here?" boomed a deep voice.

A castle guard was walking towards them. The Egg Keepers scattered into the air.

"Run!" shouted Mike.

Together the cousins raced down the slope, Autumn bounding ahead of them across the drawbridge and through the gates. The guard was a long way behind them as they entered the park.

"We've lost him!" panted Maggie.

"Keep going!" shouted Mike, weaving in and out of the trees. "Roll down this bank!"

"I'm not rolling down there!" replied Maggie, horrified.

"It's a short-cut to mine," said Mike, "my house is much closer!"

"But aren't your Mum and Dad away?" Maggie felt a little sick now.

"They're not due to leave till ten, Mike said, "Now come *on*!"

Mike rolled down the bank anyway and Maggie followed him, moving as quickly as she could.

They were all breathless by the time they arrived at Mike's house. His mother – Maggie's Auntie Lily - was standing on the doorstep. Her eyes flashed with anger. "Where on earth have you two *been*?" she said. "I've just had Rose on the phone, Maggie! We've got a plane to catch this morning, Mike, remember? What on earth were you *thinking!?*"

"I'm ever so sorry, Auntie Lily," said Maggie, "We took Autumn for a walk and we lost track of the time."

"Yeah, sorry Mum," said Mike. "It was my fault. I kept stopping to take more and more pictures." Maggie gave him a grateful look.

Mike continued, "We thought we'd better pop back here first as it was much closer and so you wouldn't all worry."

"Well come on in, both of you, and have a hot drink," said Auntie Lily. "At least you're safe and sound. I'll phone Rose and then get you some hot tea and toast."

Maggie and Mike slumped gratefully on the sofa, worn out by their adventure. Autumn flopped down by the radiator in the hall and went to sleep.

Mike's mother was just bringing a tray of tea and toast into the living room when there was a loud knock at the front door.

"Oh, whoever can that be?" she said, exasperated, as she rushed down the hall, "Oh, it's Professor Falconer!" She sounded surprised. The children heard the front door hinges creak as she opened it wide, "Stephen!" she was calling up the stairs,"Professor Falconer's here!"

Stephen Harris, Mike's Dad, came struggling down the stairs with a suitcase in each hand which he dumped on the floor.

"Good morning, Peregrine," said Stephen, "Is there something we can do for you?"

"How are my two favourite researchers?" said a sharp and spiky voice, "Just dropping off that paperwork I promised to give you in case you fancy doing a little extra work on the plane. Sorry about the early hour but wanted to be sure and catch you both before you left…"

He pushed past Lily and headed for the living room.

The children looked up as the Professor's thin beaky face appear round the door frame. "…I tend to take early trips out on my bike. Can't seem to get a good night's sleep these days at all!" The Professor turned to smile at Mike's Mum as if expecting some sympathy but she didn't seem at all in a sympathetic mood. In fact she shook her head at Uncle Stephen. *She seems really irritated,* thought Maggie. *Don't think she likes him much.* Then Maggie noticed that the Professor was not looking at Auntie Lily any more but was staring right at her. He was trying to hide a slight snarl. It was not a pretty sight.

"Ah, hello there, kiddies!" he exclaimed. Like a huge bird, he loomed over them, enveloping them in the smell of stale pipe tobacco, "Are you going to be good little boys and girls for Mummy and Daddy while they're away?" the Professor asked. "Got all your toys packed ready for your holidays?" *You're really creepy,* thought Maggie, *and you smell.*

"I'm eleven actually," she muttered.

"Actually this is my son Mike and my niece Maggie," said Mike's Dad, "They've just taken Maggie's dog for an early walk, apparently." He raised one eyebrow at Mike and winked at him.

"Bit early for little kiddies to be out, isn't it?" said Professor Falconer, smiling at them. "Now just look at that! I wouldn't mind a cup of tea and some of that delicious toast, Lily, if you've got a moment."

Mike's mother sighed heavily and went back into the kitchen. She soon came back with another cup and a plate.

"Wonderful!" said Professor Falconer, "I'll just wash my hands."

"The cloakroom is along the hall," said Stephen, "Autumn was nosing in your rucksack, Maggie," he continued, "Have you got food in it?"

Alarmed, Maggie ran into the hall just behind Professor Falconer. The Stone Egg was lying on top of Maggie's blue flowery sun hat amid the scattered contents of her rucksack! It was glowing like a lump of burning coal! The Professor's horrible pretend smile froze on his face and he strode towards it. Autumn gave a low growl as he loomed over the egg.

"Nice doggy," said Professor Falconer, stopping mid-stride and reaching out a long, bony hand towards the egg.

Autumn bared her teeth. The Professor snatched his hand back.

"I am one of the country's leading geologists, little girl," Professor Falconer hissed at Maggie. "And I want to see that rock."

"It's just a silly plastic toy - the sort that takes batteries," gabbled Maggie nervously. "I'll put it away."

Professor Falconer brought his face down close to hers. Maggie felt the hair on the back of her neck stand on end as his hot bad breath hit her.

"Now you listen to me, sweetie!" he hissed. "I suggest you give that rock to *me*!"

Autumn leaped up at him suddenly. The Professor shrieked, pushed Maggie at Autumn and then blundered back along the hall. Maggie managed to grab Autumn's collar to hold her back, then she snatched up the Stone Egg and shoved it deep into her rucksack. She slung the rucksack safely over her shoulder.

"Wretched dog went for me!" Professor Falconer was saying to Auntie Lily as Maggie went back into the living room. Auntie Lily didn't look too bothered.

"I think we ought to go now," Maggie said, still holding Autumn's collar. "We don't want to make you late for your plane."

"Alright, dear," said Auntie Lily. "Stephen, see everyone out, will you?"

"Enjoy your trip," muttered Professor Falconer under his breath, never taking his eyes off Maggie's rucksack.

You are trouble thought Maggie.

"Good to see you, Peregrine," said Mike's Dad, showing him out. "Don't worry. We'll be in constant touch with you while we're away."

The children watched the Professor climb onto the saddle of a black, shiny motorbike and drive off round the corner.

"What happened in the hall?" Mike asked as soon as they were outside. "You're shaking, Maggie!"

Maggie told him.

"He can't treat you like that," said Mike angrily. "We should tell my Mum and Dad straightaway!"

"If we did, then we'd have to tell them about all about the Stone Egg!" exclaimed Maggie. "Come on, we had better get back to my house right now!"

*****

That night Maggie dreamed she was a bird guarding her newly laid egg. It hatched into a strange creature, golden and winged, which flew high into the sky pursued by hundreds of other nameless creatures. She tried to fly in order to follow it but found she couldn't. Then she could hear someone calling her name. She woke up with a jump, realising it was her cousin Emma's voice that she could hear. *Why was Professor Falconer so interested in the Stone Egg?* She shuddered as she tried to forget the horrible expression on his face. Her thoughts were spinning and she felt terribly tired. *I just can't believe that I've been chosen by a Legend,* she thought. *I'm really worried about it.*

"Maggie! Maggie! Sid and Colin are having a spitting contest!" called Emma from the garden. "It's disgusting!"

Maggie, yawning with exhaustion, stumbled towards the open bedroom window, "They're nine year old twin boys," called Maggie, "That's the sort of thing they do!"

*****

A creature that lurked at the bottom of the deepest ocean coiled and uncoiled its tail, sounding a deep, forlorn moan as it searched the universe for a mind as cold and jealous as its own. Shoals of frightened fish darted away and hid themselves in dark corners among the coral and seaweed.

*****

"We've got to get back up to the castle," whispered Maggie to Mike later that day. "I have no idea what I'm supposed to do now."

"Plus we don't even know why the egg is sick," said Mike.

Then the doorbell rang. Maggie and Mike stared at one another. It couldn't be the creepy Professor again, could it?

"Get that please, Mike!" shouted Maggie's Dad from his office.

A coat and hat as colourful as a carnival stood on the doorstep. Inside them was Nanny Gardner, Maggie's grandmother.

"Hi kids!" she said, struggling in with a large backpack. "Take this for me, Mike, there's a good chap!"

"Hello, Rosie!" she called out to Maggie's Mum as she bustled along the hallway, "You're looking well! I knew you wouldn't mind so I've come down a day early to help out. Rick's following on in the camper van. Andrew!" she called out to Maggie's father. "Fetch my other stuff in from the car would you and be careful please! My bongo drums are balanced on the top!"

"Bongo drums…" murmured Maggie's Mum. "…Oh dear!"

"And don't forget the didgeridoo!" said Nanny Gardner, winking at Maggie.

Suddenly Nanny Gardner's mobile rang. Her ringtone sounded like someone thumping a tambourine. "Janie!" shouted Nanny Gardner into her mobile, "Yes, I made it down here safe and sound! Maggie, it's your Auntie Janie," she told Maggie, "Tell your father his sister's on the phone and would like a quick word!"

"I heard you, Mother!" shouted Maggie's Dad from his study, "Just coming!"

Mike went to bring in Nanny's stuff from her battered old car. Maggie followed him out and then decided to sneak a look at the Stone Egg safely away from the house. She opened her rucksack carefully.

"The light in the egg's just faded out again," she whispered to Mike.

"Yeah," nodded Mike, "Better put it away. Keep it warm."

"How are you, Janie?" Nanny was still shouting into her mobile. They could hear her through the open front door, "Rick and I are staying here for the whole Easter holidays to give Rose a hand! Yes, Rick's bringing the camper van because all the children are staying over so it's a full house! Yes, Lily's lot too! Baby's not due for a while yet, no!"

As Maggie listened to Nanny Gardner's booming voice a strange thought occurred to her, "Mike…you don't suppose it might be mobile phones that are killing the egg?" she whispered. "Nanny's on her mobile right now and the light went out in the egg as soon as she answered it. And remember when my Mum rang your phone up at the castle? The egg's light faded away that time as well!"

"Yeah," whispered Mike, "You might be right. What was that bit of The Legend again…'words that fill the air'…yeah…could be."

"How are Charles and the children?" bellowed Nanny Gardner down the phone. "Did Holly and David get the mobiles I sent them? They don't work? Oh, that's a shame. Well, I'll get them something else. Anyway, I'm handing you over to your big brother Andrew! Bye for now!"

Maggie's father took the phone and walked out into the back garden to speak to his sister.

"Where have you got to, Maggie?" Nanny yelled.

"Just coming, Nanny," called Maggie, her fingers tingling as the Stone Egg began to flare back into life. She shoved the egg into her rucksack and she and Mike went back in the house.

"It's a nightmare for poor Janie up in Wales," declared Nanny Gardner, "They've got no mobile phone signal at all because of the high mountains and even their landline has a fault every five minutes. They're living in the middle of nowhere!" She marched into the kitchen, "Janie's just had to use the phone box at the local pub! What's the matter with you two? Trying to catch flies?!"

Maggie and Mike shut their mouths. They were both thinking exactly the same thing. No mobiles.

"Wales!" said Maggie, when Nanny had bustled away to find the twins. "If they've got no mobile phone reception where your Auntie Janie lives, then that's *exactly* where we need to take the Stone Egg! No words that fill the air, remember?!"

*****

After lunch, Nanny Gardner's friend Rick showed up at the house, "Hello Autumn, my beautiful hound!" he said, smiling broadly, "Oh and hi there kids! Left any sandwiches for me?" Everyone liked Rick, including Nanny. She liked to play music and so did Rick. They often travelled round together, singing songs and playing all sorts of musical instruments whenever and wherever they could. Rick was hoping they could get some gigs in and around the town as they had some brand new songs they wanted to try out.

Rick dumped his bag, guitar and banjo on the hall floor. But, as Nanny shut the front door behind him, Maggie and Mike were shocked to glimpse Professor Falconer standing on the street corner. The shiny black motorbike was propped up against a brick wall beside him.

"He's followed us to your place!" hissed Mike.

Maggie's tummy felt funny. She couldn't speak.

"Rick, how are you? So good to see you!" said Maggie's Mum, hurrying into the living room. But, catching her foot on the edge of a rug, she tripped and almost fell over, twisting her ankle so much that she cried out.

"Oh no!" said Nanny Gardner, rushing over to her side. She and Rick helped Maggie's Mum back up to her feet.

"Just let me lie down on the bed for five minutes," said Maggie's Mum, "and I'll be fine."

"No, Rose, dear. You're going upstairs to bed properly. I'm here now to look after you and the baby when it comes," said Nanny Gardner firmly. "Andrew! Call the doctor right now to check that ankle!"

*****

Thursday.

Maggie's Dad and Rick were sitting at the kitchen table as the children clattered downstairs to breakfast the next morning. Nanny Gardner was busy buttering whole-meal toast.

"Where's Mum?" asked Maggie.

"Well, dear," said Nanny Gardner, "it's nothing for you to worry about but your Mum wasn't feeling very well in the night so your Dad took her to the hospital."

"They'll keep her there a little while for observation," said Maggie's Dad. *He looks rather pale and anxious* Maggie thought.

"She can come home very soon," continued her Dad, "but she's got to take it easy until after the baby's born. She'll need a lot of peace and quiet though. So we think it would be best if Nanny and Rick drive you all up to stay with Auntie Janie in Wales for the Easter holidays," he continued, "…then Mum can stay here quietly with me. Wouldn't it be great to see Holly and Dave again?" Her Dad took a sip of coffee out of his giant mug that said "COOLEST POSSIBLE DAD"

"Oooh, yes please!" said Emma, and she and the twins, Sid and Colin, started jumping up and down and clapping their hands.

"It's a wonderful idea, isn't it, kids!" said Nanny. Charles and Janie's new house is huge! Used to be an old chapel. Plenty of room for all! Maggie and Emma can come in my car and Mike can keep an eye on Sid and Colin in the camper van!" Nanny glanced at Mike, who was trying to balance a tomato sauce bottle upside down on top of a bottle of brown sauce to impress the twins, "Well, fingers crossed," she added. "I'll go and call the pub and get a message to Janie."

*****

The old white dragon sat at his desk, his head resting on his hands. He twanged his lower lip with one long finger, "Bawaaah, bawaaah, bawaaah," he went. "Now what shall I do?" he asked out loud. "Let me see, what choices do I have? I could look at the stars, or I could sit in my castle." And so he decided to walk round the outside of his castle a couple of times. "Nothing ever changes," he muttered, kicking at a small stone. "Nothing ever happens on a dead place like the moon."

*****

"That's all sorted then," said Nanny Gardner. "Come along, kids, get busy and pack yourselves enough clothes for a week please. We need to hit the road. It's a long drive."

What, now? thought Maggie. *How am I going to find time to talk to the Egg Keepers?* She glanced at Mike. He looked worried too.

"We'd better take Autumn for a quick walk first," Mike said cleverly. "Coming Maggie?"

"I took her out earlier," said Rick.

What shall we do then? thought Maggie. *There's no way Mike and I can see the Egg-Keepers before we leave!* She held her rucksack tightly.

Rick spotted the worried look Maggie shot at Mike, "Don't worry about your Mum, Maggie," he said kindly, "She'll be perfectly fine."

At that moment Maggie's Dad got up from his chair," I'm off to see your Mum in hospital now. Look after

35

those twins for me, Mike. Make sure they keep their seat-belts safely locked. No messing about."

"I will, Uncle Andrew," said Mike.

Maggie's Dad hurried out to his car.

"Now what?" whispered Maggie to Mike, "What about the Egg Keepers?"

"Look," said Mike, "The Egg Keepers believe that you will find the rest of the answers mentioned in The Legend, so I reckon you will. Fantastic luck going up to Wales, isn't it? That smelly old Professor is watching the house so at least we'll see the back of him."

"I'm glad you think I'll handle it," whispered Maggie. "It all feels like a total nightmare to me."

As Maggie and Emma settled down in the back of Nanny Gardner's car, Maggie kept an eye on Professor Falconer who was still loitering on the corner pretending not to stare at the house.

Rick started the camper van engine and Sid and Colin turned around in their back seats and stuck their tongues out at Maggie. But she couldn't be bothered to do the same back to them. She had caught sight of Mike's anxious face through the side window of the van. He was nodding at her encouragingly. As the van and the car drove off, Maggie craned her neck to look back at the Professor.

"Who *is* that peculiar man?" asked Nanny Gardner. "He's a bit old for a Hell's Angel isn't he?"

"Oh he's just the local weirdo," said Maggie. She didn't know what else to say. Then, with one last look over her shoulder, her tummy lurched again. The Professor was climbing onto his sleek, black bike!

He's going to follow us! Maggie thought.

Chapter 2

Sundews and Suspicions

"Aren't there a lot of jackdaws where you live?" Rick said as they all sat in the service station having a snack, "When I took Autumn out this morning there seemed to be hundreds."

"There are always masses of birds around," said Nanny Gardner. "You just don't go out for enough walks, Rick!" She took a big sip of tea.

"There were loads in our garden this morning," said Colin.

"Yeah…they were sitting in a long line on the back wall," said Sid, "…they were all staring at the house."

"What, *really*?" blurted out Maggie.

Everyone turned to look at her.

"I'm very interested in bird-watching," she muttered.

"So! On that subject, which one of you scribbled words all over the bird table?" asked Nanny Gardner.

"It wasn't me!" shouted the younger kids.

"Why would anyone write on a bird table?" asked Emma.

"What did it say, Nanny?" asked Maggie quietly.

"Well, it was rather strange, old fashioned, curly writing," said Nanny. "It was a poem about eggs and streams and sundews. I can't really remember now. I spotted it first thing this morning when I was doing my yoga on the lawn."

"What are sundews?" asked Colin.

"A very special plant that eats insects," said Nanny Gardner, "They grow in marshy areas where the air is very clean. Ah, now, it's coming back to me. I think it said, 'Meet us near the stream where the sundews grow' Yes, that was it, more or less."

Oh no! I've just missed speaking to the Egg Keepers, thought Maggie. *How could I have been so stupid? I forgot they can fly! I didn't need to go to the castle! I could have spoken to them in my own garden! They left me a special message and I missed it!*

"Are you feeling alright, Maggie dear?" Nanny Gardner leaned forward and put her hand against Maggie's forehead.

"I'm alright Nanny. Just a bit tired."

"Well you have yourself a little snooze in the back seat. We're going to be on the road for quite a while yet."

"I'll just take Autumn for a comfort break on the patch of grass. Get some fresh air," said Maggie. "Coming with me, Mike?"

"Sure!" Mike sprang to his feet.

They strolled up and down the narrow grass at the edge of the service station.

"I keep thinking I hear motor bikes in the distance," said Maggie, "I wish Nanny had gone on the motorway. Bikes aren't allowed."

"No sign of him though," said Mike. "This is going to be the best Easter holiday ever! It feels like I'm in a spy film!"

"I'm glad *you're* enjoying it," said Maggie crossly.

*****

A wide lorry was crawling along in the slow lane as Nanny and Rick pulled out of the service station. Nanny carefully overtook it.

"That's good," she said, looking in her windscreen mirror, "And Rick's managed to overtake it to. Reckon that lorry's got engine trouble. We'd have been delayed for ages if we'd got stuck behind that! Look at all this traffic! Must be the great Easter getaway!"

Maggie, who had spent most of the journey so far keeping her eye out for motorbikes and praying Professor Falconer would lose his way, stared once more out of the back window as they went round a bend in the road. And there he was! Yes! It was *definitely* him! All dressed in black and hunched low over the silver chrome handlebars of his horrible shiny motorbike.

*****

The creature in the icy depths of the sea snarled as it slept. Its black lip curled back to reveal rows of long, sharp teeth, as red and jagged as a rusty iron fence. A shark that had been searching for fish in the shadows changed its mind and glided away to look for its dinner somewhere else.

*****

Green forests and rusty-red mountains greeted them as they drove into South Wales.

"Look!" said Nanny Gardner, pointing up at the sky. "A Red Kite! They're protected birds, you know."

"What from?" asked Emma.

"People poisoning them or stealing their eggs," said Nanny Gardner.

"How could anyone hurt something as beautiful as that?" said Maggie, gazing out at the soaring bird. She heard its plaintive call, *peeeoooo*, and felt for a moment that she was flying with it.

"There's our signpost!" said Nanny, after a while. "*Ddraig Goch*, Auntie Janie's village!"

After a few minutes they pulled into the muddy driveway in front of a large house that looked a bit like a church. Auntie Janie, Uncle Charles, Dave and Holly came running out to meet them.

"Come inside everyone!" said Auntie Janie, "How lovely to see you all! Haven't you all grown! Get down, Autumn, you're all muddy from the lane!"

She led the way through the porch, which seemed full of rainbows as the sunlight hit the stained glass windows on either side.

"Isn't this beautiful, kids!" said Nanny Gardner "It still looks like a chapel on the outside but your Auntie Janie and Uncle Charles have turned it into a wonderful house!" She poured herself a cup of tea. "It is so kind of you to have us all out of the blue, Janie. Now then, Holly, Dave, why don't you two show your cousins round the garden?"

"No problem! Come and see my tree house!" said Dave.

"Are there many streams round here, Holly?" Maggie asked her cousin as the others all dashed off to the tree house. Where there were streams there might be sundews.

"Hundreds!" laughed Holly.

"Do you get any sundews in Wales?" asked Maggie.

"You mean like it said on the birdbath?" said Emma, jumping down from a garden wall like a fairy with her arms outspread.

"Do the sundews have teeth?" shrieked Colin, sliding down the treehouse ladder.

"And crunch up the insects and swallow them?" said Sid, jumping after him.

"What?" said Holly. "What on earth are you all talking about?"

"Streams and sundews," said Colin.

"Someone wrote about them on the birdbath at home," said Sid.

"Aaarrrggh!" shrieked Holly, "You're all totally nuts! I don't know what you're on about!"

"Sundews!" shouted Emma.

"But what *are* sundews?" shouted Holly back at her.

"Are you children arguing already?" called Nanny Gardner. "You've only just got here. I can't cope with the seven of you fighting. You need to promise to be

very good friends while we are guests in Janie's house."
She disappeared back inside.

Maggie suddenly stopped walking. Holly bumped
into her.

"Ouch!" said Holly.

Maggie had had a brainwave. She ran to catch up with
Mike who was kicking an old football about. "There are
seven of us!" she eagerly whispered to him, "Nanny
Gardner just mentioned it. We need all seven of us for
The Legend to work. It's obvious!"

"Well, you're the one the Egg Keepers chose," said
Mike, "so it's up to you to decide what to do."

"What are you on about?" asked Holly. "Why doesn't
anyone *answer* me?"

"Sorry, Holly," said Maggie. "Right. It's time
everybody knew everything. Up in the tree-house, all of
you please."

When they were all settled in the tree-house, Maggie
cleared her throat and began to explain, "A couple of
days ago, Mike and I were up at the castle with
Autumn, sitting on those big stones we always sit on
when you visit us, remember, Emma?"

"The dragon's teeth stones!" said Emma. "I love
those!"

"Before that, Maggie had been trying to make
blackbird noises with the penny whistle Nanny Gardner
gave her," said Mike.

"Yes, I was," said Maggie, "Anyway, the jackdaws
up at the castle were after our peanuts, but suddenly
they all sort of stood up, did a funny twisty thing with
their beaks, took off their bird cloaks and turned into
fairies."

"Not fairies, Egg Keepers," corrected Mike.

"Fairies?" said Dave, pulling a disgusted face.

"Wow!" exclaimed Emma.

42

"Is this from a book you read?" asked Holly, "or is it something you're making up?"

"No," said Maggie. "It's the truth. The fairies, I mean, Egg Keepers, made us walk through a hole in the grassy bank into an underground cave where they showed us a very special Stone Egg."

"Stone egg!" said Emma. "You *are* making this up!"

"Hang on, Emma, let me finish," said Maggie. "The Egg Keepers told Mike and me that the world had laid this Stone Egg but it was dying. They said they'd found me because of a special Legend, and they said all life on earth will come to an end if the Stone Egg dies."

"And so this egg's supposed to be hidden in some secret cave under the castle is it?" Dave was looking at Mike who had a very serious expression on his face. Dave knew Mike wasn't the story-telling kind. Mike nodded at Dave. "It's all true, mate." Mike said to him.

"It isn't there now," said Maggie. "They made me take it with me."

"Show us, show us!" yelled Sid and Colin together.

"So they just *gave* it to you?" said Holly, "Something that's so important that the world will end if it dies and they handed it over to *you*?"

"I know it doesn't seem very likely," said Maggie.

"Show us, show us!" chanted Sid, Colin and Emma joined in this time.

"Be quiet, please!" squeaked Maggie, "Or the grown-ups will hear us. The Legend said they need all of us children. There must be seven of us to protect it properly."

"But there's someone after it, kids!" said Mike. "Mum and Dad's boss, Professor Falconer, saw it and tried to get his hands on it. He's been following us!" He glanced over at the narrow lane that ran up to the house but there was no sign of anyone there. All he could hear was birdsong. There wasn't a hint of a motorbike engine sound at all.

Holly looked closely at Maggie's rucksack which Maggie was cradling in her arms.

"It's in there, isn't it?" Holly said quietly.

Sid and Colin's eyes widened with surprise.

"Yes," said Maggie. "It is."

She opened her rucksack, lifted out her flowery sunhat and unwrapped the Stone Egg. She held it out for all of them to see. It glowed dark red like a smouldering ember.

"Oh!" said Holly, "It does look sort of alive!"

"Now do you all believe me?" said Maggie.

"What happens now?" asked Dave. He looked rather serious.

"I don't know," said Maggie. "We had to leave before the Egg Keepers could tell us what to do next."

"Do you think that man is still following you?" asked Emma, looking over her shoulder.

"We can fight him!" shouted Colin, punching the air.

"Yeah!" said Sid, jumping up and joining in.

"Ssssh, boys, stop it!" said Maggie. "We haven't seen him since the service station. But that doesn't mean he's not still around."

"Well," said Holly, "If someone is after this egg, you need to hide it. What are you going to do with it?"

"The Egg Keepers didn't tell us anything else," said Mike.

"But they left us a message on the bird bath at home about eggs and sundews and streams," said Maggie, "Nanny Gardner saw it but I missed it."

"And don't forget the meadow pipits," said Emma.

"The what?" exclaimed Maggie, "*What* meadow pipits?"

"The message also talked about them," said Emma. "Nanny said they are a kind of bird."

"Why didn't you say anything before, Emma?" Maggie exclaimed.

"Nanny would have thought I wrote it and told me off," said Emma.

"Can you remember *exactly* what it said?" asked Maggie.

"Yes," said Emma. "When will the Stone Egg wake? The meadow pipits know. You must meet them by the stream where the sundews grow."

"Oh Emma, that's fantastic!" said Maggie, leaning forward to give Emma a hug. "So now we know we need to find sundews, streams *and* meadow pipits!"

"It doesn't help much," said Mike. "I wouldn't recognise a sundew if it bit me on the ankle, or a meadow pipit for that matter."

"Maybe there are sundews quite close by. There are loads of little plants by the stream at the back of the field right here,"suggested Dave, "Mum's got a book that talks about all kinds of plants and wildflowers. We could look at a picture of a sundew so we know what we're looking for."

"Will you take us there tomorrow, Dave?" asked Maggie.

"Dinner's ready!" called Nanny Gardner from the back porch. "Then it will be an early night for all of you. It's been a *very* long day."

*****

Maggie lay awake for a long time that night. When she did sleep, she dreamed that she was on the top of a mountain, holding the Stone Egg. Coming towards her was a dragon. As she stretched out her hands to show

45

the egg to the dragon, a huge bird with long talons came swooping down out of the sky, snatched the egg and carried it off in its claws. The dragon spread its wings and Maggie just managed to scramble onto its back as it chased after the bird, but then she slid off it again and was falling...falling...falling between branches of trees that brushed against her with a horrible scraping sound. Far below, coming nearer and nearer, was a cascading river, crashing over rocks.

Maggie drew in her breath to scream and then suddenly woke up. She sat bolt upright in her bed. The scraping sound was actually Autumn scratching at her bedroom door!

Maggie took Autumn downstairs in case she woke up Emma and Holly. Quietly, she let the dog out into the shadowy garden. The dog rushed towards the tree house and then jumped around the tree, growling. Maggie had to whistle to her several times before she would come back. Worryingly, Autumn refused to settle down for the rest of the night.

*****

The creature on the distant sea-bed flexed its fingers, its purple claws slicing like shards of glass through the piles of slimy seaweed on which it lay.
Hundreds of tiny crabs as pink as babies' toe-nails scuttled away to bury themselves in the silver sand.

*****

46

Good Friday.

  The smell of frying bacon and eggs woke Maggie, Emma, Holly and Autumn. They ran down the spiral staircase to the back kitchen.

  "Dad, someone's been in my tree house!" Dave was saying to his father.

  "Weren't you all up there yesterday?" asked Uncle Charles.

  "No! I mean someone *else*," said Dave. "It smells all smoky and all the cushions were bunched up in one corner."

  "I'll go and have a look," said Uncle Charles.

  "Plus all my train books were knocked over," said Dave.

  "No-one's going to bother to touch your silly old train books," said Holly. "Mum, can we go up to the reservoirs on the post bus? We could take a picnic!"

  "Those books are not old *or* silly," said Dave giving his sister a hard stare.

  "What did Nanny Gardner say yesterday about arguing?" reminded Auntie Janie.

  "Can't you children just amuse yourselves in the garden today?" said Nanny Gardner.

  "It's Good Friday Bank Holiday," explained Auntie Janie, "No post buses running today, I'm afraid."

  "Well, then, would it be okay if we climb up the little mountain at the back?" asked Maggie. This was a golden opportunity to seek out the streams, sundews and pipits!

  "Oh, I don't know about that," said Nanny. "Do you think they'll be safe, Janie? I'm not happy with them going off on their own up a mountain."

"Oh, they'll be fine," said Auntie Janie. "It's the one you can see at the end of the garden and it's more of a hill than a mountain. My two go up there all the time. Dave never gets lost and Mike tells me he's done loads of outdoor stuff with the scouts haven't you Mike? All the kids round here go out to play on the hillside all the time."

"Okay, then," said Nanny Gardner, "But you older kids take good care of the little ones."

*****

"Listen, all of you," said Dave, as they headed along a rough road beside the field towards the mountain that was really only a hill, "Someone was definitely in the tree house last night. It stank of tobacco smoke. Look, I found this." He fished a crumpled piece of shiny paper out of his pocket. Maggie took it and smoothed it out.

"Mike look! It's that photo of Grandma and Granddad Greenwood with both our Mums when they were babies!" she exclaimed.

"It's exactly like the one off our mantelpiece at home!" answered Mike, "How weird is that!"

"Autumn was making a terrible fuss about something in the garden last night," said Maggie. "Who could have got hold of that photo?" But even as she said it aloud she already knew the answer. The memory of the smell of tobacco smoke from Professor Falconer came back to her from that day when he had tried to take the egg. He had failed to take the egg, but had stolen the photo instead!

They continued to trek up the lane that wound gently across the hill slopes.

"So, where's this stream, Dave?" asked Mike.

"Over there…" said Dave, pointing at a tiny stream gurgling among the rocks and gorse bushes. They all ran over to it and Dave pointed down to the ground, "…I checked Mum's book. This is a sundew, look!"

They looked but, at first, couldn't see anything amongst the many green plants at the stream's edge. Then Maggie exclaimed, "Oh, yes, I see them! You mean those tiny red ones!"

"Oh, yeah!" chorused Sid and Colin, who both knelt down to take a closer look.

"I thought they'd be bigger than that!" observed Sid.

"And where's all the sharp teeth?" asked Colin.

"They're very sparkly," said Emma, peering at them. "Really lovely and sparkly like diamonds."

"So," said Maggie, "here's the stream with sundews. All we need to find now are some meadow pipits. Let's sit down and wait and see if they come. Can you tell me what The Legend said, Mike? My mind's gone all blank."

"When the Stone Egg cannot glow for all the words that fill the air, then comes a maid who you will know by the moonlight in her hair," said Mike.

The rest of the kids all stared at him.

"We reckon words that fill the air means all the millions of words transmitted on mobile phones," said Mike importantly.

"We think they are what must be killing the egg," added Maggie, "And the moonlight bit is about my silvery blonde hair." She could feel herself blushing when she told them this last bit. It sounded sort of stupid to say it out loud to other people. But it was the truth after all.

"Mobile phones don't work round here," said Dave. "It's because of all the mountains. The mountains block the signals from the phone masts. It's a real pain."

"We know that," said Maggie, smiling at Mike. "That's why we're here!"

"We've worked out some other bits of The Legend too," said Mike. "Bells that don't ring – they're bluebells, reddish shades - that's Autumn, singing like blackbirds means Maggie's penny whistle…"

"Wearing flowers that will not fade," said Maggie, "That's probably the flowers printed on my sunhat, we decided. Then there was another bit about roses and gardens and woods."

"From gardener and from rose, from ancient greenwoods she descends, something like that," said Mike.

"Which is me," said Maggie. "You see, my name's Gardner and Mum's name is Rose. That means me!"

"And our Mums were called Greenwood before they met our Dads and got married," said Mike. "So that means Maggie's descended from the Greenwoods and so am I!"

"And so am I!" Emma pointed out. "It's not all about *you,* Mike! And so are the twins for that matter!"

"Yes, so are *we!*" piped up Sid and Colin.

"Alright," said Maggie, "yes, you are. We're all related to one another in some way. I'm sure that's important and why it has to be us seven. And then there is the really gloomy bit about me having to rescue the Stone Egg or else the world will die."

"Don't forget the stuff about dragons which sounded pretty cool to me!" said Mike.

"And rainbows in caves I suppose," admitted Maggie.

"Wow!" said Holly. "Rainbows in caves!"

"Look!" whispered Emma, pointing at the banks of the stream. "Loads of really little birds have arrived!"

They all sat very still. Small, streaky brown birds were flying down onto the grass near the water's edge.

They had white sides to their tails and a pale stripe over their eyes.

"Shame they aren't jackdaws," whispered Maggie to Mike, "I was hoping to see more Egg Keepers."

"They must be the meadow pipits," Holly said under her breath.

"Does that mean they can't be Egg Keepers?" asked Emma, "Are Egg Keepers always jackdaws?"

"Duh!" said Mike, slapping his forehead. "If the Egg Keepers disguise themselves as birds, they'd have to be the right sort of birds for the area wouldn't they? It's obvious!"

"Well I assumed they'd always be jackdaws too," said Maggie.

"Think about it", said Dave. "It would be no good the Egg Keepers deciding, 'Oh, I know, today we'll disguise ourselves as penguins and go and sit in Trafalgar Square,' or 'let's dress up as sea gulls and take a stroll along the mountain tops', now would it?!"

"Ssshhh!" hissed Maggie, "You'll frighten the meadow pipits away!"

Quite a crowd of pipits had gathered by the stream now. Suddenly, all together, they flicked their left wing tips up to their throats and twisted off their cloaks and beaked hoods. In the deep silence, the children could hear themselves breathing.

"Fairies..." whispered Emma, amazed.

"No. Egg Keepers..." whispered Maggie.

One of the Egg Keepers stepped forward. She had streaky brown hair which hung around her shoulders like a cloak. She wore a pale yellow tunic and long pink boots shaped like birds feet. Her wings shone like stained glass windows.

"I am *Chikka*," she said. "*Chark* and his friends sent news to us that you were coming. You've brought the Stone Egg with you, Maid Maggie?"

"Yes," said Maggie. She liked being called Maid Maggie in front of all the others. She rested the Stone Egg carefully on the grass. *Chikka* flew over to it.

"It looks well," said *Chikka*, "I think it will survive."

"Well, that's good, but please could you tell me what happens now?" asked Maggie.

"It is our Earth's child," said *Chikka*. "Our Earth bears a child like this every ten thousand years. Soon the egg will begin to hum."

"Then what happens?" asked Maggie.

"It will rise into the air, growing bigger and bigger as it rises," said *Chikka*. "Water will flow from the cracks and crevices on its surface. Rivers and seas will form. Fish will swim in the waters. Trees and plants will spread all across the land. Animals will appear. Birds will fly in the skies. Then, when it feels the time is right, the Stone Egg will travel out into space and become a brand new world."

"Oh wow!" said Mike.

"That's amazing!" said Holly and Emma.

"Fantastic!" said Dave.

The twins just stared at *Chikka* in surprise with their mouths wide open.

"If this happens regularly," said Dave, "why wouldn't we have heard about it before?"

"Maybe you should check your history books more carefully," said *Chikka*. "There have always been stars that men have followed. They have been written about and painted in pictures and woven into tapestries."

"What's a tapas tree?" asked Colin. "Is it like a burrito?"

"When's the egg going to do it then?" asked Sid.

"Yeah, when will it shoot up into the air?" asked Colin.

"When it is ready," said *Chikka*.

"I've got so many questions for you," said Maggie. "But my mind has gone totally blank. I can't even remember any of The Legend. Please, *Chikka*, tell me what we, The Seven, must do now?"

"Now," said *Chikka*, "you must go to meet the Dragon Speakers."

"Who are they?" asked Maggie.

"They were in The Legend ," said Mike. "I remember them. Are you going to take us to them?"

"No," said *Chikka*. "The Dragon Speakers are the Guardians of the Night. They will not speak in daylight. What's that?" *Chikka* sounded alarmed. There was a loud roar, and they turned to see a black motorbike bumping down the mountain path towards them.

"We must depart! Be ready, Maid Maggie, an hour before sunset tomorrow," *Chikka* called.

The children turned back to where the Egg Keepers had been standing. A flock of meadow pipits were flying over the stream and across the hillside. Soon they were just specks in the distance.

"Everybody hide!" shouted Maggie, grabbing the Stone Egg and shoving it into her rucksack.

"Follow me, kids!" yelled Dave.

They ran down the bank to a clump of gorse bushes and lay down flat behind them.

The motorbike stopped on the rough track. Professor Falconer took off his inky black helmet and scanned the hillside. He had a huge golden eagle on the back of his leather jacket. He took out an enormous pair of binoculars from a case around his scrawny neck, scanned the horizon then climbed back on his bike and roared off down the mountain path leading away from the children.

"Phew, that was close!" said Mike. "I don't think he saw us. That was definitely him, Maggie!"

Why does Professor Falconer want the egg so badly?" thought Maggie. *What does he want to do with it?* She didn't want to worry the others, but they would be bound to ask questions sooner or later.

"This way, kids. Better get going…" said Dave.

They walked down a different path through an oak wood, finding themselves ankle deep in drifts of pale pink wood anemones. A little tired by now, they sat down by the edge of a little pool over which enormous bright blue dragonflies skimmed.

"They're just like tiny helicopters," said Emma.

"Seems early in the year for dragonflies," said Holly, "Don't they usually hatch out in summer? Everything's all topsy-turvy since your fairies showed up."

"Didn't like that eagle man much," said Sid.

"Me neither," said Colin.

The white dragon stopped muttering and staring at the cold black sky. "Woo-hoooo!" he exclaimed, doing a little dance as he chanted.
"I've done it! I know how many stars there are! I know, I know, I know!"

He shimmied back through his door and sat down at his desk. With a flick of his wrist he flexed his fingers and dipped his claw into the ink. "What will I write today?" he thought, watching with interest as his hand moved across the page.

And he wrote…

Primal Soup

The world is born. Around the sun she spins.
And in the steamy swamp a change occurs.
Now in the murky water something stirs.
The sun smiles down as life on earth begins.
To get this far has taken many, many years.
Now the time has come for things to change.
The mountains shake. The world is feeling strange
And from the ground a new Stone Egg appears.
It starts to glow. It floats up into the air.
It hovers, waits, instinctively it knows.
The baby dragons fly to meet it there.
It rises up and into a new world grows.
Heading off into space - a bright new earth,
Our planet's child. Our world has given birth.

"I wonder where all this poetry comes from?" the white dragon thought. "It just seems to appear in my old, wise head." Wandering out of his door, he stood still for a moment looking at the stars as horror struck him. "No!" he shouted, his voice like shingle scoured by waves. "I've forgotten the answer to how many stars there are! I should have written it down!"

*****

When they got back home Dave said, "I'm going to bring all the cushions and my train books in from the tree house. I've got a feeling that old biker bloke was sleeping up there the other night. Are you sure we shouldn't tell our Mums and Dads about all this? My parents are really into ecology and saving the world. I'm sure they'd understand."

"I'm sorry, Dave, but we can't," said Maggie quietly, "Sometimes I wish we could." She looked very tired and worried indeed, "I honestly don't know what we are going to do about the egg now."

"How can the rest of us help you out, Maggie?" asked Holly kindly.

"Well, I suppose we'll need to be in the garden, pretending to play so we don't miss anything. Dave, Holly, you'll need to think of an excuse about why we need to be out for a couple of hours around sunset." said Maggie.

"Grown-ups always want you home when it starts getting dark," said Emma.

"Star-gazing!" suggested Holly helpfully. "Dave can teach us all a bit about stargazing! He's very good at spotting all the constellations and things."

"Brilliant idea little sis!" exclaimed Dave. "But we still won't be able to stay out for long."

57

"I wonder what the Dragon Speakers live," said Emma. "We might have to walk a long way, mightn't we?"

"I expect it will be somewhere near the little mountain…" said Maggie thoughtfully, "…so we had better take some torches."

"I hope we see the Stone Egg rise!" said Colin.

"It's going to be awesome!" said Sid.

None of them woke in the night when Professor Falconer climbed up to the tree house and found it bare, chilly and empty of comfy cushions. And none of them heard him getting up very early, shivering till his teeth rattled, and slinking away in search of a warm café and a hot breakfast in the village. Autumn had woken up just once, disturbed by the hooting of a night-owl, but worn out by that day's adventures she simply sighed and went straight back to sleep.

*****

The creature that lurked at the bottom of the sea twitched its ears as if, even in its fitful sleep, it was listening. It ground its teeth together with silent fury. Its eyelids rolled as it watched something in its dreams. Sea anemones that had set up home in its cavernous ears edged to the outside and, releasing their hold, let the tides take them to whatever fate lay beyond.

*****

Easter Saturday

"Let's all go out to the garden to plan things," said Maggie. "Can you remember the rest of The Legend, Mike? I need to be ready for anything. I know there is a rainbow and a cave…"

"In the Dragon Speakers cave, a rainbow she will meet," said Mike.

"Not a cave!" said Emma. "I hate caves!"

"So do I," agreed Maggie, "but we'll all be together and we're going to find a rainbow, Emma, imagine that!"

"The maid has got to save the Seven," said Mike, "but I can't remember the other line."

"For the magic cycle to complete," said Maggie. "I'm sure that was it."

"And we are the Seven!" stated Sid proudly.

"Will it be dangerous?" asked Colin a little nervously, "Why do you need to save us?"

Maggie was not at all sure what to say about this. "Mike and Dave will look after you," said Maggie. She nodded at Dave who nodded back. His Mum and Dad had thought the star-gazing lesson was a brilliant idea. He had even promised he would bring all the kids safely home by 7pm. He really hoped that he would prove himself to be their brave protector. "Got your torches everybody?" he asked.

"Yes!" they all replied.

"Look!" said Emma. A flock of birds were swooping low across the grass.

"So many feathers!" exclaimed Holly.

"Just like snow!" shouted Colin, running after the birds. Laughing loudly, Sid joined in too. Emma followed them, dancing among the feathers that the birds dropped from their beaks. The tiny feathers landed in a winding line that seemed to lead towards the small mountain at the back of the field.

"They're telling us we've got to get back to the mountain," said Maggie, starting to run. "Come on, everybody!"

Through the back gate, across the field full of goats, and up the narrow track the line of feathers led them. Occasionally they lost the trail but then they would spot a few scattered feathers a bit further on until, finally, they arrived at the top of the mountain that was really a hill.

"I'm tired," complained Emma, "and I've got a stitch."

"You'll be fine," said Mike, "The trail of feathers has stopped. We're obviously exactly where we're supposed to be."

And he was right. The narrow line of feathers stopped right in front of an enormous pale grey rock.

"So, where to now?" asked Dave.

"I don't know," said Maggie. "I don't understand what they want us to do next."

"Look!" said Colin.

"Bats!" said Sid.

Sure enough, as the sun was setting, tiny bats were appearing one by one, darting silently above the gorse bushes.

"Do they bite?" said Emma. "I don't like bats one little bit!"

"They won't bite you," said Mike, "They usually just hang upside down in caves. They find their way through the air with a sort of radar."

"They're really clever!" said Sid.

"What's radar?" asked Colin.

60

But Dave didn't get the chance to explain for, just then, a bat landed right at Emma's feet. She squealed with shock.

"Don't be afraid children," squeaked the bat in its strange, high voice. "I have been waiting for you. I am *Barglor*, King of the Dragon Speakers!"

Chapter 3

Chocolate Eggs and Chases

Barglor was a tiny man about seven centimetres high, with large pointed ears and rather jagged teeth. His skin was golden brown, his eyes were inky black, his clothes were of soft, dark velvet, including his cloak, and his feet were long and bare with very sharp toe-nails.

"The Dragon Speakers are *bats*!" exclaimed Maggie.

"We are *not* bats!" spat *Barglor*, angrily pulling himself up to look taller.

"Are you the same as Egg Keepers?" asked Emma.

Barglor spat again and flew up into the air.

"We are the Dragon Speakers, the Guardians of the Night," he said. "The Egg Keepers are Guardians of the Day. We do not mix with one another. We do not speak. We keep our own perfect laws. I am the Chief Dragon Speaker. It is I who will take you to talk to the dragons."

"Sorry?" said Maggie. No-one had said anything recently about actual dragons.

"Now we're talking! This is getting better and better!" said Mike, excitedly. He grinned at Dave but Dave was watching *Barglor* with a very serious expression.

"Do you not know that all the mountains and hills of the world are dragons?" hissed *Barglor*.

"I don't see how they possibly can be," said Dave, "I'm sure in geography books it says…"

"No, we didn't know that," interrupted Mike. "Proper, living dragons?!"

"*All* of the hills and mountains?" asked Holly, staring at the horizon where the land met the sky.

"*Look*, you can see dragon shapes on those mountains over there!" said Sid.

"Yeah! The nearest end is its nose and the other end is its back," said Colin.

Emma frowned at the twins and then at the mountains and hills. She didn't see any dragons in their shapes at all. Holly put her arm round her. "They're curled up, Emma, just like Autumn when she's asleep," she said.

"So are the mountains *sleeping* dragons then?" asked Maggie, puzzled.

"Oh, no!" hissed *Bargl*or. "They're certainly not asleep. They don't move around much but they are wide awake I assure you."

"Mountains can't move at all," said Dave, "or people would *see* them. Surely you'd notice if a mountain got up and walked around!" He was starting to wonder if he had made the right decision to help Maggie out in this weird adventure.

"Sometimes one of the older dragons in the deeper levels will fall asleep," rustled *Barglor*. "And, if he dreams it causes an earthquake."

"Oh yeah?" said Mike. "Then it's lucky they don't have nightmares!"

Maggie scowled at him. Mike was being very silly and she could feel herself getting cross.

"They do!" squeaked *Barglor*. "I am telling you the truth! An angry or frightened dragon breathes fire hot enough to melt rock!"

"Ah, I see what you mean now. I think you are actually describing an erupting volcano," said Dave.

Maggie said as politely as she could, "Please, sir. What has all this got to do with the Stone Egg?"

"Has no-one told you the destiny of the Stone Egg?" asked *Barglor*.

"Well, the Egg Keepers said it is the Earth's egg. It starts to hum, then rises into the air, then goes far out into space to become a brand new world," said Maggie. "They said all the dragons follow it there."

Barglor made tutting noises. "Typical of them," he hissed, "not mentioning the importance of our part in it all. Keeping all the glory for themselves. When the Stone Egg begins to hum, Maid Maggie, it sends a signal to the dragons that it's time to lay their *own* eggs."

"Mountains laying eggs?" said Maggie, raising her eyebrows. This was getting crazier by the minute.

"That goes against all the laws of physics," said Dave.

"I think it is high time for you to meet the dragons," squeaked *Barglor*. "They will wish to tell you the way of things themselves. I hope you have you brought the Stone Egg with you, Maid Maggie?"

"Yes," said Maggie.

"Very good," hissed *Barglor*. "Then there is no time to waste. Follow me. It will soon be getting dark."

Emma began to whimper a little and took hold of Holly's hand.

Barglor flew over to a large rock and a huge cloud of squeaking bats followed him. Then an opening appeared in the rock and all the bats flew in.

"This way!" called *Barglor*.

Dave and Mike shone their powerful torches into the cave opening. Then, with Maggie and Mike leading the way and with Autumn and Dave at the back taking care of the younger ones, they all stepped through the hole in the rock one by one.

Don't think about it, thought Maggie, taking a deep breath. *It's only a tunnel and you're not on your own. All the Seven are here. You mustn't let the little ones see you're scared.*

"Follow me quickly," *Barglor* squeaked. "Your eyes will soon become accustomed to the darkness!"

The seven children stumbled forward, clinging on to each other's hands and jumpers and feeling their way along. Emma kept treading on the backs of Maggie's shoes in her eagerness not to lose her. They could feel the temperature dropping as they struggled down a steep slope. The ground under their feet was slippery and the walls were wet and rough.

"I'm frightened, Mike..." Emma whimpered.

"Pretend it's a game, sis," said Mike. "They do this sort of stuff all the time in the scouts. It's about being a good team."

Holly took hold of Emma's hand.

The twins weren't scared at all. They were really enjoying themselves making troll noises, grinding their teeth together and growling.

Why does it always have to involve tunnels and caves? Maggie thought. *I can face anything better than tunnels and caves.*

"It's not much further, children!" squeaked *Barglor*.

Then a creaking voice near Maggie's ear whispered, *"They won't let you out."*

"What? Who said that?" exclaimed Maggie, stopping in her tracks and looking around anxiously.

"Who said what?" said Emma.

"Oh nothing," said Maggie, not wanting to frighten her. "I just thought I heard something."

"They control the doors," said the voice to Maggie.

"You'll become like us," said a different voice, and Maggie thought she heard it chuckle.

"Who are you?" whispered Maggie.

"Everything okay, Mags?" asked Mike.

"Yes, fine…" said Maggie, trying not to tremble.

"Stand still everyone!" *Barglor* hissed. "Turn left, take two steps, and left again. Stop!"

They all stood blinking as their eyes adjusted to the brightness. They had entered a vast cave. The ceiling rose far above their heads, curving like a bubble. Every inch of the cave was encrusted with crystals of every colour imaginable. Tiny rainbows flickered inside the crystals, filling the whole cave with light.

"Wow!" they all said together.

"It's like being inside a kaleidoscope!" said Holly.

"The Legend said I'd meet a rainbow in the Dragon Speakers' cave," Maggie spoke softly as she craned her neck to see the ceiling.

"We're right inside the mountain…" said Sid in his best troll voice.

"Deep underground…" snarled Colin in his spookiest voice.

"Mum and Dad would love this," said Mike. His parents were both scientists and collected fossils. That was probably why their horrible old boss, Professor Falconer, was chasing after Maggie's Stone Egg. He must have thought it was an unusual specimen!

"Yes, remember that special rock on Dad's desk," said Emma, "like an ordinary old stone until he broke it open and found it was full of crystal."

"This is the heart of the Rainbow Mountain," announced *Barglor*.

It felt like a great cathedral. Bats hung like gargoyles from the walls. Stalactites and stalagmites were joined together to form gleaming white columns at the back of the cave.

They look like just like church organ pipes, thought Maggie. In front of them was a huge green slab of rock crystal. *Barglor* flew over to it and settled there.

"This is the Cradle Stone, children," *Barglor* said. "Please step forward."

They walked slowly across the cave, seven tiny figures under the vast, echoing dome. Autumn lay down and watched them anxiously.

"Please, each of you, touch the stone," said *Barglor*.

The huge green stone felt cool and smooth beneath their finger-tips. Then suddenly the cave began to vibrate. Autumn whimpered a little as a breeze stirred the air. A deep voice seemed to rise up from beneath their feet.

"There are seven of you here!" it boomed. "And the beast you call Autumn!"

"Waaah!" exclaimed Holly, grabbing Dave's arm.

"It's only adrenalin making you feel shaky," whispered Dave to his sister. "We just did the effects of shock on the body in Science." But he was feeling pretty shaky himself!

"Quiet! You are about to speak to the dragon of the Rainbow Mountain," rasped *Barglor*.

Emma edged a bit closer to Holly.

"Are you a real dragon?" Colin asked, shouting up into the ceiling space.

"Why can't we see you?" asked Sid staring into the clear green depths of the Cradle Stone.

"Because you are standing inside me," rumbled the deep voice. "We dragons are the hills and mountains. We are the rocks, we are the ground beneath your feet, we are the caves and we are the tunnels!"

"Even the cave where I got the Stone Egg?" asked Maggie.

67

"That castle is built on the back of a dragon," intoned the voice, "The Stone Egg was inside the dragon's mouth."

"So those stalactites, were they the dragon's teeth?" asked Mike.

"Correct!" boomed the voice.

Maggie remembered the bad smell and the slime in the cave. She shuddered.

"We must speak to the one who has brought us the egg," rasped the voice.

"That's me...I've got it here," Maggie stammered.

She rested the Stone Egg in the centre of the Cradle Stone. She realised she was trembling and her legs were having trouble holding her up. *I don't want to be doing this,* she thought. *I wish Mike had been chosen. He's loving every second of it!*

"Please tell me what happens now?" she asked politely.

"This is the fulfillment of the Stone Egg's destiny," echoed the voice. "When it begins to hum, we lay our own eggs. When it rises, the dragons' eggs hatch. Then the baby dragons fly up to meet it, curling around it, forming many mountain ranges. The dragons will merge with the Stone Egg, forming a new world as it travels far out into space."

"Ooooh!" whispered Holly.

"How lovely..." breathed Emma.

"*Chark* said the world would end if the Stone Egg died," said Maggie.

"The dragons cannot love the Earth if we cannot lay our eggs," intoned the voice. "Without our love the Earth would freeze and life would cease."

"How exactly do you *know* life would cease?" asked Dave sensibly.

"It has happened before." The booming voice shook the Cradle Stone. "Many thousands of years ago, meteor dust and volcano smoke killed the Stone Egg. We were angry with the Earth. She should not have allowed her precious egg to die. Many of the dragons left and then the Earth froze."

"And life on Earth disappeared?" persisted Dave.

"The dinosaurs died," intoned the voice. "We were extremely sad for them."

"Maybe it wasn't the Earth's fault," suggested Maggie timidly, "Maybe she couldn't help it."

"It was certainly not *our* fault," echoed the voice, shaking the cave, "Enough questions! Go now! Tomorrow, at this time, when the Stone Egg begins to hum, you must all return!"

"Thank you," said Maggie, not knowing what else to say. "Umm…do I leave the Stone Egg here now?"

She really hoped so. The responsibility was starting to weigh her down.

"The dragons have spoken!" said *Barglor*. "Leave the egg here where it belongs! I will guide you safely back to your home."

Maggie squared her shoulders and took hold of Emma's hand. *Barglor* flew a short way ahead, flipping over in the air from time to time to watch the children and make sure they were alright. Maybe she had imagined those horrible voices whispering, *"You'll be trapped for ever. They control the doors. You'll become like us, like us, like us…"*

Barglor flipped over in the air and said, "Stop! Turn right, take four steps. Now turn left!"

She was surprised and relieved, then, to find they were stepping out of the bank into the field of goats. The field was bathed in twilight and the stars were beginning to sparkle over their heads. They looked round for *Barglor* but he - and the hole in the bank - had completely disappeared.

"Wow…" said Dave, checking his orienteering wrist-watch, "We've only been gone for thirty minutes!"

"Seemed like hours!" said Holly.

When they arrived home they peeped through the kitchen window and could see Nanny Gardner, Rick, Auntie Janie and Uncle Charles all seated around the wood-burning stove. It looked like they were drinking Nanny's famous hot chocolate with sprinkles. Nanny Gardner turned her head, spotted them and waved cheerily.

"Back already?" she shouted, "Come on in and join us!"

*****

The creature in the deep dark waters of a faraway ocean opened eyes as wet and red as raspberry jelly and its eyelids hung in folds like dark blue suede. It looked furiously about, as if searching for a terrifying enemy. It began to swish its tail to and fro. Several starfish tiptoed casually away over the sand until they were out of range of that dangerously flicking tail.

*****

"Space is a silent, lonely place," mumbled the old white dragon, as he slumped in his chair. "Silent!" he shouted, his voice straining and cracking at the unfamiliar exercise. "Silent! SILENT!" He ran round the outside of his castle waving his arms about.

70

"AAAARRRGGGHHHHH!" he yelled. "SO
SILENT!!!"

His words hung like bubbles in the emptiness of space
before floating aimlessly away. "Must get on," said the
old white dragon…And he wrote…

The Dinosaurs

One morning, sixty million years ago,
The dinosaurs smelled hot volcanic smoke.

The ones the lava missed began to choke.
Meanwhile another egg began to grow.
The Egg rose up. It felt the blistering heat.
It tried to breathe that air so thick and black.
Now it had been born it could not go back.

The world lay covered by a sooty sheet.

The dragons raged. Their eggs remained un-
laid.
They would not give their brood so poor a
start.
They blamed the earth for this mistake she'd
made.
Some chose to stay, but many to depart.
The Stone Egg fell to dust. Its mother cried.
The dinosaurs lay in the dust and died.

*****

Easter Sunday

The village green was full of excited children. An
important looking woman in a flowery dress had just
made a little speech through a squeaky microphone,
telling the bigger children to help the little ones follow
the bits of coloured ribbon in order to find all the Easter
eggs that were hidden nearby. The Easter Egg Hunt was
on!

Maggie was deliberately standing away from the
others by a hedge on one side of the village green. It
was fun and busy and cheerful but she was not feeling

72

any happy feelings to speak of. She needed to be alone to think. But, just as she turned to stroll back across the green, she was horrified to see Professor Falconer's beady little eyes staring right at her. He lifted up the visor on his motorbike helmet even further and she saw that his face was full of bad temper.

"Found you at last, sweetie…" he said through his yellowing teeth, blocking her way back to the others. "You've led me a fine dance, haven't you?"

"Get out of my way!" shouted Maggie, recoiling as his bad breath hit her face.

"That's not likely to happen, sweetie, now is it? I have chased you and your little friends all over the country," said Professor Falconer, "I've even had to sleep in a rickety uncomfortable tree house two nights running. I'm not spending good money on a bed and breakfast hotel – the university doesn't pay me enough!"

"Ask them for a wage rise then!" said Maggie. "And find something better to do with your time. Time you're wasting, by the way!" There were crowds of people everywhere so she felt safe and brave enough to speak up and stand her ground.

"Wasting my time, am I? Is that so? Now you listen carefully to me," he stooped down and loomed over her. She could clearly see the vicious hawk logo printed on his motorbike helmet. "I'm a *very* powerful man at that university, understand? I'm in charge of your cousin Mike's Mummy and Daddy… AND I WILL SACK THEM IMMEDIATELY FROM THEIR JOBS IF YOU DO NOT LET ME HAVE THAT EGG AT ONCE!"

He was yelling at the top of his voice. A few people looked over in their direction to see what on earth was going on.

73

"I *have* to get that egg you dear, kind little girl..." continued the Professor. He had noticed the people staring and was now trying to change his voice from angry to kind, "I can't go home without it or I will get into very big trouble with the university. Please give it to me and I'll leave you alone, I faithfully promise." But although his voice was softer, his eyes had taken on a wild, hawkish look and a nerve had started twitching in his cheek.

Then, all of a sudden, there was Nanny Gardner, puffing her way towards them across the grass.

"Oi!" she shouted to Professor Falconer. "Get away from my grand-daughter! What are you playing at?!"

Maggie had never seen Nanny Gardner look like that before. With her wild curly hair and brightly-coloured clothes, she was a startling sight indeed! Her green eyes flashed with anger as she grabbed the Professor by the arm.

"Police!" she shouted. "Police! This man is bothering my grand-daughter!"

"Really, Madam," protested Professor Falconer, giving a high-pitched laugh. "You're entirely mistaken. I am known to her cousin's parents. They are my employees. I was merely trying to chat to the little girly - whom I have met before at her cousin's home by the way - in a friendly fashion. More importantly, I am sorry to have to inform you that this child has stolen an important egg specimen that belongs to *me*."

The village policeman was running over the green towards them, followed by Uncle Charles, Auntie Janie, Rick, and the rest of the children.

"This man..." said Nanny to the out-of-breath policeman, "...is trying to tell me that my grand-daughter has stolen his Easter egg! I've never heard anything like it!"

"No, Madam, you don't understand…" spluttered the Professor.

"Trying to take Easter Eggs from children, are we, sir?" said the policeman, "Got a bad chocolate habit have we? I think you'd better come with me don't you? You and I need to have a little chat."

"No! You don't *understand*," said Professor Falconer, rolling his eyes. "I'm the leading geologist in my field! She's stolen a very important and rare fossil specimen which is *mine*!"

"As I just said, sir, we shall talk about it down at the station," said the policeman. And he led Professor Falconer away, who was still protesting at the top of his voice.

"Whatever next!" said Nanny Gardner to the crowd. "Trying to steal Easter Eggs from innocent children - that horrible man!"

"Are you okay, Maggie darling?" asked Auntie Janie.

Maggie nodded, "He's just a bit mad I suppose, " she said quietly.

"Yeah. Loopy." Mike helpfully made a loopy sign over his own head. He and Maggie looked at one another. They both knew they shouldn't tell the grown-ups too much but they had to tell them something.

"Mike and me do know him a bit though. He's not exactly a stranger," added Maggie, staring hard at Mike.

"He's Mum and Dad's new boss at the university." said Mike. "They can't stand him. He keeps sending them off on geology field trips all the time, like he wants them out of the office."

"How very odd," said Auntie Janie, "Well he's obviously a little bit wacky. Poor old Lily and Steve – how do they stand to work with him?

"What's gee-lolly-gee?" asked Colin.

"Old stones stuck in mud," replied Sid.

"I think it's high time we all went home," said Nanny Gardner.

*****

The village policeman called in to see them later that afternoon.

"Professor Falconer won't be bothering you any more," he told them. "We've sent him off to the main police station thirty miles away. They're going to get a doctor in to take a look at him. He's telling us he's been under a lot of strain at work lately. Eccentric kind of bloke, isn't he? Terrible bad breath."

All the children exchanged glances. Maggie was praying they would all keep quiet. They did.

"What's egg centric?" piped up Colin, breaking the silence.

"Not normal," replied Sid.

Maggie knew she had some quick thinking to do. After they had all finished their 4 o'clock cups of tea, she said, "Is it okay if we all take Autumn for a quick walk? It's such a lovely sunny evening."

"Oh, I don't know about that, Maggie," said Nanny Gardner, looking anxiously at Auntie Janie, "Not after what happened today."

All the children held their breath.

"The policeman did say that they'd sent the old weirdo out of the area," said Dave. "Mike and me will look after everyone. We'll be fine, don't worry."

"Well," said Nanny Gardner, "just as long as you're careful. Once round the fields at the back and home within an hour, okay?"

Maggie called Autumn to her side and all the children left the house, walked down to the end of the garden, through the field of goats and then headed up the mountain path as quickly as they could.

"Let's see if we can find where we came out of the mountain last night," said Holly. But although they searched high and low, they couldn't find the entrance anywhere.

"We'll have to go the long way round then," said Maggie. "Even though we've only got an hour, we'll have to risk it."

"Aren't the Dragon Speakers sweet?" said Holly. "I can't wait to see them again"

"They're bat-men!" giggled Sid spinning round with his arms spread out.

"Super heroes!" shouted Colin, trying to spin faster than Sid.

"Ssshh!" laughed Emma. "The Dragon Speakers will be cross if they hear you being silly."

"They don't come out during the day, remember?" said Colin.

"They're 'Guardians of the Night'," said Sid, chuckling and pulling a spooky face.

"I think they're sweet too," said Emma, "with their little pointy ears and spiky teeth."

Colin made another face that showed his teeth, "Like vampires!" he yelled, and he and Sid chased Emma across the field, hissing and flapping their arms.

"I think I like the Egg Keepers best," said Holly, "they're so happy and they look like little flowers."

"It *was* the mad Professor up in the tree house then," said Dave, "and he definitely stole that photo off Mike and Emma's mantelpiece that day he dropped round."

"Yes," said Maggie, "But at least we've got rid of him for now."

"But why is he so keen to get his hands on the egg?" asked Dave. "He seems completely determined."

"I don't know," replied Maggie. "But what I *do* know is that if he *does* find it, everything will be ruined. Come on everyone, walk a bit faster. The dragons said we need to be there when the egg starts to hum. We'd better hurry up and get to the big grey rock."

Maggie knew she had to be determined. She decided there and then that she would not be nervous any more. And, as they made their way up the mountain path, she was almost managing to convince herself that she had only imagined the strange whispering voices in the tunnels.

They found the big grey rock and sat down beside it.

"I can hear a noise," said Holly.

As they all listened, they could just make out a very faint low note that seemed to be coming straight up through the ground underneath them.

"It's the Stone Egg!" shouted Sid.

"Yes!" cried Colin. "It's humming!"

*****

Beneath the sea, the creature lifted its head, flared its nostrils as it sniffed the water then licked its lips with a tongue as black and sloppy as a slug. It pricked up its ears, which stood to attention in the water like two enormous indigo lilies as they listened to a humming sound far away.

*****

Maggie gave a small scream as something landed on her shoulder.

"Good evening," said *Barglor's* squeaky voice in her left ear.

"*Barglor*," she said. "You made me jump!"

Barglor chuckled.

"It is time, Maid Maggie," he said. "The Stone Egg is humming."

"Yes, we can hear it," replied Maggie.

"What happens now?" asked Mike.

"Come with me," said *Barglor*. "The next stage has begun.

They set off once more into the tunnel that led to the crystal cave and, although Maggie listened very carefully, she didn't hear the whispering voices again. *I really must have imagined it,* she thought.

The humming pulsed like the heartbeat of a huge animal, filling the cave. As they walked towards the Cradle Stone, flashes of white were flickering across the Stone Egg's surface like sunlight catching ripples of water in a clear stream.

"It looks happy," said Holly.

"What happens now?" asked Emma. "Is it dangerous?"

"You will come to no harm," said *Barglor*. "The dragons wish to honour you."

The Cradle Stone trembled as the dragon's voice boomed out.

"Every tenth millennium," it roared, "when the baby dragons fly away to meet the Stone Egg, seven dragons remain behind. They are the new generation that will become all the mountains on Earth. So, at the next tenth millennium, it will be *their* eggs that will fly first to meet the next Stone Egg. The dragons wish to honour you seven special humans by giving these seven special eggs into your keeping."

"Thank you," stammered Maggie. *Oh no, not more eggs to look after!* she thought secretly.

"Dragons eggs!" whispered Colin.

"For us!" gasped Sid.

"Cool!" said Mike.

"We have been warned by Our Legend that our eggs will be in danger. We need you to guard them," boomed the dragon's voice. "They are the Seven Eggs. You are the Seven Guardians.

"Is that the same Legend that the Egg Keepers told me about?" asked Maggie.

All the Dragon Speakers stared at her. Some of them hissed, showing their pointed teeth.

"The Egg Keepers told you The Legend?" squeaked *Barglor* at the top of his voice.

"Yes," said Maggie. "Was that wrong?"

"They do what they want," said *Barglor*. "They are the Guardians of the Day…"

"Yes, I know all that," interrupted Maggie. "But why don't you like each other?"

"The Egg Keepers are not governed by the dragons," said *Barglor*, "They obey the wishes of the Earth. The dragons answer to no one."

"Many thousands of years ago," boomed the dragons' voice, "when the Stone Egg and the dinosaurs died and we could no longer lay our own eggs, the Earth was lonely. She knew how angry we were. And so she created her precious Egg Keepers to guard future eggs. And that is why the Egg Keepers believe that it was not the Earth's fault."

"We do not associate with the Egg Keepers," said *Barglor*.

"But that's really sad," said Maggie. "Seems to me you all want the same thing. For the earth to be alive and healthy forever and ever until the very end of time."

"You are a wise child indeed, Maid Maggie, but not all questions have simple answers," said *Barglor* softly.

"Have you ever tried to talk to the Egg Keepers?" asked Holly.

"*They* have never tried to talk to *us*," said *Barglor*. "Why should we bother?"

"Before the Egg Keepers," boomed the dragon, "the dragons had the Earth all to themselves."

"So the dragons are jealous of the Egg Keepers then?" said Holly.

"But the Egg Keepers are here to help the Earth!" said Emma.

"The Earth should not *need* the Egg Keepers," said *Barglor*.

"Is the Earth jealous of the Dragon Speakers?" asked Holly.

"We are necessary!" shouted *Barglor*. "That is all you are required to know!"

"Well, anyway," said Maggie, "please tell us what we have to do to save the seven dragons' eggs. Where are they at the moment?"

"They have not yet been laid," roared the dragon's voice, "The Stone Egg is humming. Tomorrow the first of the seven eggs will be laid. Every day for seven days one of the seven eggs is laid. You must find them all, guardians, for there are others who would harm them."

Maggie and Mike looked at each other. They were both hoping that Professor Falconer was still thirty miles away at the police station.

The cave stopped vibrating. It was perfectly silent. The dragon had gone.

"That gives us seven days, counting today!" said Dave, "You're heading home next Sunday, Maggie!"

"What day is it now?" asked Mike.

"It's Easter Sunday," said Maggie, her voice getting higher. "Dave's right. We all go back to school next Monday!"

Barglor cleared his throat. "It is important above everything else that you find the seven eggs as quickly as you can," he said. "Clues will be sent to you. Secrecy is vital. Spies are everywhere."

This is getting ridiculous! thought Maggie. *I thought once we'd got the Stone Egg away from all the mobile phone waves, it would rise. We've managed that and now we need to save seven more dragons' eggs in seven days! We've got no chance!*

"Danger threatens everywhere," *Barglor* continued, "There are evil forces at work. We need you to keep the seven eggs safe and get them to the Rising Place."

"Oh, right! And where exactly is the Rising Place?" snapped Maggie.

"You'll know it when you see it," said *Barglor*. "I will show you to the green bank now so that you can return very quickly to your home," and he led them safely back through the tunnels.

"Tomorrow…" *Barglor* called to them as he flew away, "…the first egg will be laid. Be watchful, guardians!"

*****

Easter Monday

After breakfast, Sid and Colin were out in the garden looking for twigs to make bows and arrows.

"Look at that little bird…" whispered Colin. "It flies to every spot I stare at - watch!" He moved his head to stare at a different branch.

"They're like the ones on the bird table at home," said Sid. "Nanny calls them greenfinches. Oh, look, it flew when you turned your head. I saw it!"

"I know!" said Colin. He turned his head a few more times back and forth.

"Wow!" said Sid. "Why is it doing that?"

"I don't know," said Colin, sitting on a tree stump, his eyes fixed on the greenfinch.

Sid sat beside him. The greenfinch cleared its throat.

"It might be an Egg Keeper," hissed Sid.

"It's singing," whispered Colin. "Listen."

And the greenfinch sang:

Green the woodpeckers, green the trees.
Green the broccoli, spinach and peas.
Green the water-melon skin.
Green the grass snake, long and thin.
Green the seaweed on the rocks.
Green the grass stains on your socks.
Green emeralds in a jeweller's shop.
Green lizards, newts and frogs that hop.

This egg is licked by a tongue that's green,
Nearby herbs grow for king or queen.

The little greenfinch bowed to the twins.

"This is your first clue," it said. "You must go and search for the first dragon's egg today." Then it fluttered its feathers and flew away.

Sid and Colin looked at each other with very round eyes and ran off straightaway to find the others.

"Can't you remember it all?" said Maggie when they told her about the greenfinch.

"It was a very long poem with snakes and frogs in," said Sid, "And lots of other green things."

"There were lizards," said Colin. "And something with a green tongue."

"And kings and queens and verbs," said Colin.

83

"Not verbs - herbs!" laughed Sid. "Like what Mum sprinkles on the pasta!"

"What on earth has a green tongue?" said Dave, frowning.

"If it said Kings and Queens…" said Holly thoughtfully. "…there is a sort of royal house around here. We visited it with my school class once. Not too sure about the herbs though. But they do have a vegetable garden with greenhouses."

"We'll ask Nanny Gardner and Rick to take us there!" suggested Dave, "We can tell them it will be very educational!"

*****

"We want to find the vegetable garden, Nanny," Maggie said, after they had finished walking round the stately manor house.

"Yes, we're *very* interested in herbs actually," agreed Emma.

"What animals have green tongues, Rick?" asked Sid.

"I've no idea," said Rick. "Some lizards might, but I can't be certain."

Nanny took them to the high-walled vegetable garden at the back of the manor house.

"Here are your herbs, girls," said Nanny. "That's comfrey over there - it was used years ago to treat aches and pains. These are foxgloves, not in flower yet, but you can see the leaves. Foxgloves were an old treatment for heart problems before we had all our modern drugs. Some of the things we use today still come from herbal remedies. You have to study for years to know what plants to use and how to use them properly.

Let's sit down everyone and I'll tell you the story of the old manor house while we eat our picnic."

Rick, who had brought his guitar, started to play a very beautiful tune. And then Nanny Gardner began her tale:

Once upon a time, many hundreds of years ago here in this village, there lived a poor shepherd boy who used to graze his sheep beside a lake, high up in the mountains. One day, whilst sitting on its shores, he saw ripples breaking on the surface and suddenly, out of the water walked a beautiful girl. Her dress shimmered like mother-of-pearl and her hair shone like moonbeams. She walked over to where he sat and smiled, then turned and walked back into the lake...

"Didn't she say anything?" asked Emma.

"Not a word," said Nanny Gardner.

"Unusual for a girl," said Mike. "Watch it!" he added, as Holly flicked a spoonful of trifle at him.

"Anyway, as I was *saying...*," said Nanny, frowning:

The shepherd boy fell in love with the beautiful girl and decided that he wanted to marry her. He came back to the same spot next day and waited. Sure enough the water rippled again and the girl walked out of the lake. The shepherd boy was very shy and didn't know what to say, so he handed her a piece of his bread. The girl took the bread and bit into it.

"It's too hard," she said and walked back into the lake.

The shepherd boy was very upset and went home to make some more bread. This time he baked it in the oven for less time so that it was much softer. The next

85

day when the girl appeared, he gave her some of the soft bread.

"It's too chewy," she said and walked back into the lake."

"This is like Goldilocks and the Three Bears," said Sid.

"Did the Princess look like a bear?" said Colin, shrieking with laughter.

"Anyway, as I was *saying…*" said Nanny Gardner, glaring at them:

The next day when the girl appeared, the shepherd boy was very sad because he had nothing else to give her, so in desperation, he gave her a piece of bread that he'd dropped into the water on the edge of the lake.

"Ugh!" said Holly.
"Yuk!" said Emma.

The girl took the bread and ate it, continued Nanny Gardner. *When she had eaten it, she smiled at the shepherd boy.*

'Thank you,' she said.

He was so delighted that he stammered "Will you marry me?"

The beautiful girl said, "If my father says I may."

Then she turned and walked back into the lake.

"I wouldn't marry someone who gave me a dirty old piece of bread that he'd just dunked in a lake," said Holly.

"It's a wonderful story," said Maggie. "I like it."

But the story wasn't over yet. Nanny continued:

The next day, the shepherd boy went back to the lake. This time, when the girl came out of the lake, she was not alone. Instead of one girl, there were three identical girls. With them was a tall man with flowing white hair and long blue robes. He wore a golden crown. He was the King of the Lake. He spoke to the young man.

He said, "I bring my three daughters to you. If you can tell me which one of my daughters you love, I will grant you permission to marry her."

The shepherd boy said, "This is the one I love." He took one of the girls by the hand. He knew her by the clasp of river-pearls that she wore in her hair...

Mike made a loud kissing noise on the back of his hand and grinned at Dave.

"Do you want me to finish this story, or not?" said Nanny Gardner crossly.

Dave and Mike blushed red and looked hard at the grass.

"Thank you very much, now as I was *saying*," said Nanny Gardner.

The king said, "You have chosen correctly. I will allow you to marry my daughter, but you must understand one thing. You must never hurt her. If there comes a time when you have hurt her three times, she must return to the lake."

The shepherd boy was horrified. "I will never hurt her," he told the king.

"Very well," said the king, and he turned and walked back into the lake.

His other two daughters followed him. From the waters of the lake walked a herd of fine cattle of purest white. They went and stood beside the girl.

87

"A present from my father," said the girl.

And so they were married. They were very happy. They had three fine sons and became very rich because the herd of cattle produced the finest milk for miles around. Then one day, as they were walking to the cow shed, one of the cattle ran towards them. The shepherd, afraid that the cow would knock down his wife, pushed her out of the way so that the cow would not run into her. His wife looked at him with tears in her eyes.

"Husband," she said, "you have hurt me."

"But he was *saving* her!" shouted Holly. "That's not fair!"

"Let's see shall we?" said Nanny, smiling at Holly:

The years went by. One day, they were at a wedding. The shepherd's wife began to cry. The shepherd was embarrassed that his wife should cry at a wedding. He tapped her sharply on the shoulder and told her to be quiet. His wife turned to him.

"Husband," she said sadly, "that is the second time that you have hurt me."

"But *why* was she crying?" asked Emma.

"She said that she could see great sadness in the future for the couple who were getting married," said Nanny Gardner, and continued…

One day, they were attending a funeral. The shepherd's wife kept laughing. The shepherd was upset. He tapped her on the shoulder, and asked her to stop laughing as it was disrespectful.

She said "I am happy for the dead person because he is no longer in pain. But you have hurt me for the third and last time. I must return to the lake."

The shepherd begged his wife to stay but she left the church and walked back to the lake. All the snow-white cattle followed her. They walked into the lake behind her and the shepherd never saw his cattle or his beloved wife again...

"That's so sad!" exclaimed Emma.

"Is that the end of the story?" said Colin.

"Not quite…" continued Nanny Gardner:

The shepherd's three sons all grew up to be fine young men. Before she had returned to the lake, their mother had taught them herbal lore- which is how to cure people of their illnesses using herbs and plants. They all became great doctors, the most famous in the land. And their sons became great doctors after them, and so on and so on...

"Wow!" said Holly.

"It's a rather silly story," said Dave. "What's the point of it?"

"I used to think that too when I first visited this place," said Nanny Gardner. "Then I noticed just how many herbs grow around the manor house and throughout the village for that matter. And then I read all the names on the headstones in the churchyard. There are many, many names there, all from one family, some going back hundreds of years. And many of those people were physicians.

"What's a fizzy-shin?" asked Colin.

"A kind of doctor," Rick replied.

"If you look in the doorway of the church there is a memorial to one of the most famous Physicians in the family," said Nanny.

"People don't really come out of lakes just like that," said Mike, "It wouldn't be possible without an aqualung or a snorkel."

"Oh, I don't know about that," said Nanny Gardner. "You'd be surprised at what could happen in the ancient times of the folk tales and stories."

"Well, if there's a *real* lake here, can we go and see it?" Dave said.

"Yes! We might see the Lady of the Lake ourselves!" shouted Emma, excited.

"It was hundreds of years ago, Emma," said Mike sarcastically, "Even if the story was true, she'd be dead by now!"

"People like that are immortal," said Holly dreamily.

"The physicians in the family even treated the King of England," said Nanny Gardner. "It was all recorded in a book. It says so on the notice in the church."

"Really?" said Maggie. She was wondering if there might be a clue to the greenfinch's instructions hidden in the church.

"That's right," said Nanny, "But I think it looks a bit too much like rain to risk going to the lake. Let's pack up and get back to the van and head for the church!"

*****

As they drove away from the manor house, the sun faded away behind a dark cloud and, just as Nanny predicted, the rain began to pour down. By the time they reached the next village the countryside was dripping wet and smelling as fresh as a daisy as brand new sunshine sparkled on the trees and hedgerows. Rick parked the van by the church.

"Everything's so bright green and beautiful now!" exclaimed Nanny, "Look at those hart's tongue ferns up on that bank by the graveyard, nestling in among the comfrey and foxgloves!"

"What?" said Maggie, looking closely at Nanny Gardner. "*What* sort of ferns did you just say?"

"Hart's tongue," said Nanny Gardner. "A hart is a deer. Over there, look. They're exactly like great big green tongues."

"Green tongues…" repeated Sid and Colin, looking straight at Maggie.

"Can I have a closer look, Nanny?" asked Maggie.

All the children crowded round the ferns as Maggie reached her hand deep in to the middle of the clump of shiny green leaves. She searched around quickly but there was nothing to be found.

"No luck," she whispered to the others. Rick and Nanny were busy tidying up the picnic rubbish from the van and putting it into a litter bin by the roadside.

"Let *me* look," insisted Colin, reaching deep into the ferns. He pulled his hand out again quickly and thrust something into his pocket. He winked at his big sister.

"The church is locked, sorry kids!" shouted Rick from the church porch. "Best get back in the van again everyone!"

The children scrambled back into the van and put their seat-belts on in silence.

"You are a funny lot," said Nanny Gardner. "One minute as noisy as a flock of magpies, the next as quiet as mice. Let's explore some more, shall we?"

As they drove on through the hills and mountains, Colin slid his hand into his pocket and lifted something out onto his lap. The others craned their necks to look.

"What are you children up to in the back?" said Nanny. "Have you all got your seat belts on?"

91

"Yes, Nanny," they chorused.

Colin turned to face the others and pressed his fingers to his lips. He held out his hand to show them a tiny bright green egg. It wasn't a perfect egg shape oval like the Stone Egg. It was slightly longer as if someone had stretched it like a rubber band. A bit like a very sad teardrop as it runs down a cheek.

They all suppressed gasps of amazement. Emma pressed her clenched fists up to her mouth in order not to squeal with delight. The egg shone like emerald sunlight through green beech leaves.

"Crocodile eggs look a bit like that," whispered Mike.

"What was that Mike, dear?" boomed Nanny from the front seat.

"Er, nothing…just saw a funny looking pub sign…" replied Dave.

Maggie silently gestured to Colin to put the green egg in her rucksack.

"I'll keep it safe until we get home," she whispered to him. She was so delighted to have found the egg that she decided to play her penny whistle on the journey home.

"That's such a pretty tune, Maggie," said Rick.

"She gets her musical talent from me," said Nanny Gardner proudly.

*****

The white dragon stepped back to admire his handiwork. "Rather good," he said. "Yes, that's really rather excellent," he added as he walked around the dragon that he had created, sand-castle style, out of the thick white dust. He faced the dust dragon, and swept it a low bow. "How do you do?" he croaked. "And how are you?" The dust dragon stared back at him silently.

92

"Aaarrrgghh!" said the old white dragon, and he kicked the dust dragon which disintegrated instantly. He scuffed the dust smooth with his foot. "All nice and tidy again," he said with a sigh, crossing back to his desk. And he wrote…

The Ice Age

The earth was cold. Not many dragons chose
To stay with her when all the others went.

Without her coat, the earth could not prevent
What happened next. And so she shivered.
Then she froze.
She was very angry for she was not to blame.
She had not caused volcanoes to erupt.
She didn't know how wicked and corrupt
was one old dragon's nasty, jealous game.
For years she lay, wrapped round with ice and
snow.
She felt so sad the dinosaurs had died.
And what had killed her egg? She didn't
know.
Then came the day the earth broke down and
cried.
Her tears were warm. The ice began to thaw.
The earth became a living world once more.

*****

"I bet we've not seen the last of old Falconer," said
Mike as they all headed up the mountain. They had
always managed to get back within an hour from
Autumn's evening walk and so the grown-ups seemed
happy to let them go out. But Maggie dreaded them
saying 'no' one evening. She would have to sneak out
on her own if that ever happened.

"They couldn't just lock him up," said Maggie,
"They'd have to be able to charge him with something."

"Being ugly on a motorbike?" suggested Dave
helpfully.

"I can't believe I found a dragon's egg!" yelled Colin, skipping round in circles.

"Fantastic!" said Sid, turning a cartwheel.

"Funny how you found it, Colin, when Maggie had already looked in the ferns before you," said Holly.

"It found *me*," said Colin. "So did the greenfinch."

"I'm going to try to talk to *Barglor* about the Dragon Speakers' and the Egg Keepers' silly argument," said Holly. "They need to make it up and be friends."

"Oh, please don't, Holly," said Maggie. "*Barglor* may get cross."

"Hide!" hissed Mike, suddenly grabbing Maggie's shoulders, "Get down everyone! I can hear something!"

They all ducked down in the middle of a clump of gorse bushes. They heard bracken scrunching, bushes rustling and then a man's voice muttering.

"Did you see who it was?" asked Maggie when the noise stopped.

"No," said Dave, "but it seems to have gone now. It was just someone out walking, I expect."

"Ouch!" shouted Colin, as *Barglor* landed on his head. Bats landed all around them.

"I hear that you have found the first dragon's egg," said *Barglor* hanging on to Colin's left ear. "Guard it well. One will appear every day for a week."

"Hello, *Barglor*," said Maggie.

"*Barglor*, I want to talk to you," said Holly sternly. "I think the Dragon Speakers should make it up with the Egg Keepers."

Barglor flew straight up into the air with a loud spitting noise and disappeared. The other bats flew after him.

"Oh, Holly!" said Maggie. "I told you not to tell him that! I wanted to show him the green egg!"

"Sorry," said Holly. I only wanted to help."

"He knows you've got it safe, Mags," said Mike, "I suppose we might as well get back as soon as possible."

"Yes…" agreed Maggie, "Somehow I don't feel safe with it up here."

"Did you hear that?" said Emma. "I thought I heard voices coming from over there!"

They all listened carefully, but everything seemed quiet.

"Where are we going to hide the little green egg when we get home?" asked Holly as they walked down the mountain path.

The bracken rustled with stealthy footsteps. A stone dislodged by an unseen foot rattled down the slope. They stood still and listened but, again, everything was silent.

"Sheep." said Dave reassuringly. But everyone knew it wasn't.

They walked home in silence, waving to Rick who was preparing his folding bed in the camper van which was parked in the driveway. Rick loved sleeping in his van. He was a man of the outdoors, Nanny always said.

They trooped into the kitchen.

"Can we all go up to my room and play?" asked Holly.

"That's a good idea, darling..." mumbled Nanny Gardner who had been fast asleep in an armchair by the wood-burning stove,"...but play quietly please, I'm worn out."

Holly's room contained a small stained glass window which had once been in the wall behind the chapel alter. Janie and Charles had moved it carefully upstairs when they were doing all the building works and changing the chapel into a house. The shimmering light from the rose-shaped window made everything flicker with a changing patterns.

"I *love* your room, Holly," said Emma. "It's like you've trapped a rainbow."

"It's a great place to hide the egg," declared Maggie, "because there are so many different colours in here no one will notice it!"

And so they rested the dragon's egg on the shelf beneath the rose-shaped window among Holly's collection of shells and coloured glass ornaments.

"If you want to hide something put it in full view," laughed Dave.

"We've got to find *seven* before we go home, remember?" said Maggie anxiously.

Dave went over to the shelf and gazed at the egg.

"I wonder how big the dragon will be?" he said. "This is really not much bigger than a quail's egg!"

"Chicks grow really fast," said Sid. "I expect dragon chicks do too."

Maggie smiled, but she was still very worried deep inside. Sid could well be right!

*****

The creature thrashed its tail in a rage. The surrounding sea cringed before crashing back to fill the gap. Sailors said they had never known such a squall. The creature snorted great snorts that drew in gallons of water along with many startled sea creatures unfortunate enough to be nearby. Then it gushed them out of its nostrils like fish soup, turning the water pink and cloudy for miles around.

*****

Tuesday

Next morning, Nanny Gardner and Uncle Charles were down in the garden.

"Come out here at once, children, please!" called Nanny, "Have any of you kids been kicking a football against the wall of the house right here?" She was pointing to the sprawling roots of a large wisteria vine which looked as if they had been quite badly trampled. The vine led straight up to Holly's bedroom window.

The children all shook their heads.

"Are you sure?" asked Uncle Charles, "That trellis has taken quite a bashing. I'm going to have to replace it."

"It wasn't any of us, Dad, honestly," said Dave. Dave had a serious look on his face, Maggie noticed.

They were obviously both thinking the same thing. Someone knew the dragon's egg was in the house.

"One last chance everyone," said Charles, "Are you absolutely sure none of you did this? Honesty is always the best policy."

"What's the police got to do with it?" said Colin, but no-one could be bothered to correct him.

"I believe them, dear," said Nanny Gardner to Uncle Charles, "They're good kids. They're telling the truth, I'm sure of it. It might well have been badgers rooting about or even that massive farm cat trying to hide from Autumn. Now off you all go everyone, and play nicely."

Once the grown-ups had gone back inside the house to consider matters, Maggie took all the children to one side. She didn't want to scare the smaller kids so it was important to at least look as if she was in complete control. "I suggest we make the tree house our meeting place each morning," she said to the others, "We have to try and stick together now. It's *very* important."

They all headed off to the tree house and gathered by the wooden ladder that led up to its broad wooden platform. But no one, including Maggie, quite knew what to do next. Everyone, even the younger children, were thinking the same thing. *Who* had trampled the wisteria vine and broken the trellis under Holly's window?

Suddenly a robin flew over to sit on the top rung of the ladder. Sid held out his hand. The robin flew to him and landed on his outstretched fingers. Sid stood very still, hardly daring to breathe.

"Quiet, everyone..." whispered Maggie.

Everyone held their breath.

They all stared at the robin as it began to sing:

The sky is red when the sun sets at night.
The coal glows red when the fire's alight.
The coral grows blood-red under the sea.
Your blood is red if you cut your knee.
Cheeks can go red and so do cold noses,
In summer gardens grow ruby-red roses,
Strawberries, raspberries, plums and cherries.
At Christmas the holly has bright red berries.

Red is the egg that comes with a sting
A friend will show you the rusty wing.

"This is your second clue," chirped the robin, and he gave a little bow before flying away.

"Oh, wow!" gasped Sid. "Did you see what he did?"

"Well," said Maggie, "It looks like you're supposed to find the next egg for us, Sid. But where on earth shall we go to look for it?"

"Rusty wings…where are we going to find rusty wings?" murmured Dave thoughtfully.

"Some old statues have wings…" said Mike. "Where's the nearest statue to here?"

"I know! Wales is full of old statues of *dragons*!" shouted Holly. There's got to be one round here, on top of a roof or on a gatepost or on a flag or something!"

"But it says we're going to get stung!" cried Emma, "I don't want to be!"

"Let's take a walk around the village," said Maggie. "If we can't see anything obvious, we'll have to think again."

As they walked towards the village green, they stopped to peer over the bridge into the gurgling river. Holly pointed downwards.

"Look," she said, "There's a thrush down there that's hurt its wing."

"We can get through that gap there and down the bank," said Mike. "Don't make a noise or you'll scare it. Everyone be very quiet."

They crept along the riverbank to the bird which was holding its wing crooked, but as soon as they got near, it shook itself and flew away.

"Oh," said Maggie. "It seems fine after all." She turned round to go back up the slope."Get down!" she hissed suddenly, ducking her head. They all huddled together.

"What is it?" whispered Mike.

"Ssshh!" hissed Maggie, and pointed up at the bridge.

The other children peeped round the wall. Crossing the bridge were two people, a man and a woman. They both wore black leather jackets and carried motorbike helmets.

"We're close to finding them," the man was saying. "I'm not giving up now after we've come this far. The Professor won't pay us our fee if we fail."

The children crouched as low as they could and kept very still. The couple disappeared into the distance.

"More bikers!" exclaimed Holly.

"Yes," said Maggie. "Did you hear what they said? They're following us. The Professor must have hired them to help him!"

"If we hadn't come down here after that injured bird," said Dave, "we'd have walked straight into them."

"Except it wasn't injured," said Maggie. "It was warning us."

"Do you think *all* the birds are helping us, then?" said Emma.

"Birds, or Egg Keepers," said Maggie. "Yes, they're definitely helping us."

"How are we supposed to find the next special egg then?" asked Holly.

"I haven't got any idea," said Maggie. "I've been watching all the birds around us just in case. If they really are helping us, I expect they'll guide us to it somehow. Let's go to the post office and ask if there are any dragon statues around that we don't know about."

The lady in the post office was very helpful and showed them several dragon statues and ornaments in her local guide books, but they were all a very long distance away.

"Oh, but I was forgetting. There's a lovely red Welsh dragon on a great big flag on the roof of the bee farm down the valley," the lady said.

"Bees!" exclaimed Emma. "I don't want to be stung by bees!"

"Red is the egg that comes with a sting…" chanted Mike.

"Sorry dear?" said the lady in the shop.

"Nothing," said Maggie. "Come on everyone!"

A red kite bird circled above their heads as they walked towards the bee farm. It kept crying "*peeeooo... peeeooo...*" and occasionally swept down almost to the ground.

"It's not going to hurt you," said Maggie when Emma clutched at her hand. "Look at how pretty it is with its big rusty red wings. Oh! It's just dropped a feather!"

She let go of Emma who ran forward and knelt down in the long grass.

"Mind…" Maggie warned. "Those are nettles." But Emma still plunged her hands into the middle of the nettle patch.

"Ow, ow, ow!" Emma cried out, pulling her hands back quickly. But she was triumphantly holding up a great big rusty-red feather.

"There's something else in there!" Sid said and clenching his teeth, he bravely put his hand into the nettle patch. He withdrew his hand with a jerk, struggled to his feet and uncurled his fingers to show them what he'd got. He was holding a tiny ruby-red egg. They all gathered round to admire it. The red egg shone like a sunset in the palm of his hand.

"The red kite," said Dave. "Of course! I never thought of them as having rusty wings. Well done, Sid!"

"I've stung my hand a bit but it was worth it," said Sid.

"Me too," said Emma, looking a little tearful.

Maggie searched around for a dock leaf. Where there were nettles there were usually dock leaves too. "Here we are," she said to Sid and Emma as she picked two broad glossy dock leaves, "Rub your hands with these. It will take the sting away. You were both very brave."

"For you, Maggie," said Sid, proudly handing Maggie the shining red egg.

"Let's go up the mountain…" said Maggie, putting the egg and the red feather carefully into her rucksack. "We'll try to find *Barglor*."

"He won't be about during day time," said Mike, but the others were already running across the field.

"I'll race you!" shouted Colin, running ahead with Sid and Mike.

As Mike bounded up the mountain that was really a hill, he suddenly held his hand out to stop the others following him. Turning round, he put his finger to his lips and gestured to them to go back. They edged back down the path to a flat grassy area.

"What's the matter?" whispered Maggie.

"There's a tent…" whispered Dave. "I can see that man, the one we saw on the bridge, cooking on a camping stove. You all wait here with Mike. I'll go back and have a closer look."

"Be careful, Dave," whispered Maggie.

Dave crept back up the slope. He was only gone for a few minutes but it seemed like a lifetime. Then he reappeared, running and sliding down the slope.

"Go!" he said, and they all ran and jumped back down the steep path.

"What happened?" asked Maggie, when they all paused to catch their breath.

"The woman, the other biker, came out of the tent and looked straight at me," said Dave. "I'm sure she recognised me."

"Falconer's spies…" said Mike, dramatically.

"What do we do now?" said Holly. "Why did they have to pick that place to camp?"

"Dave said, "It doesn't mean we can't still meet *Barglor*."

"Yes, we just have to sneak round the other way," said Maggie, "We've got to get to *Barglor* and warn him about the spy bikers. I think we should tell him we're being followed. If we get split up, we'll meet by those tall trees down there, okay?"

They crept through gaps between gorse bushes and rocks, crawling on hands and knees, sometimes freezing in their tracks when Dave held his hand up and only moving when he signalled that it was safe.

"We're going to gather over there by the big grey rock," Dave whispered, "and wait for *Barglor* or the Egg Keepers. Nobody make a sound."

They were just settling down in the hollow behind the rock, making themselves as small as possible, when a gruff man's voice rang out.

"Hey there, guys! We've been looking everywhere for you!" It was one of the spy bikers!

The children reacted instantly. They ran in all directions, scattering down the hillside.

Maggie was dragging Emma by the hand. She decided to hide the two of them behind a big fence post in the field of goats.

She heard a loud yell, carefully turned her head, and glimpsed the two spy bikers out of the corner of her eye. They looked very angry and confused, as if they didn't know which child they should be chasing. Then they split up, one jogging up the lane towards the village and the other running down a sheep track. Maggie's heart was thumping in her chest. Dave was with Holly and Mike had dashed off on his own. But where on earth were the twins?

Just then, Sid and Colin and Mike came crashing through the trees and raced into the goat field. They were gasping for air. They stood in the shelter of the goat pen, clutching their sides and listening.

"Think we lost them!" said Mike. "This way's quite well hidden among the gorse. They wouldn't be expecting us to leave the main path!"

"Sid," said Colin, "Why did you yell?"

"*Barglor* landed on my head," said Sid. "He made me jump. He said, "You've found the egg. Guard it well. Danger is all around.Then he flew away."

"Stating the obvious I reckon!" said Mike.

"There go Dave and Holly, heading straight for the house!" cried Emma.

Maggie sighed with relief. All the guardians were safe again.

"What do we do about the two bikers, Mike?" murmured Maggie, "They obviously know where we live."

"I don't know, Mags, I really don't," replied Mike, "But everything seems to have got a bit scary and serious all of a sudden."

Chapter 4

Spies and Surprises

The white dragon walked in through the front door of his castle. "That was interesting," he said. "It's been very many centuries since I went for a walk, but it all looks much the same as it used to."He sighed and sat down at his desk. "Now, where was I?" he thought. He scratched his long nose with one sharp claw. "Ice," thought the white dragon, as ideas played like a film in his mind. "I've never felt ice." He glared over his shoulder out of the window. The stars looked innocently back.

*****

The children took the red egg back to the house and put it with the green one on the shelf beneath the window. Sid arranged some of Holly's brightly coloured plastic jewellery all around them.

"Fantastic camouflage!" Dave said, "Well done Sid!"

"Maggie! We called your Mum on the pub phone this afternoon!" shouted Auntie Janie who was coming up the stairs. Sid quickly stood in front of the green and red eggs to hide them.

"How is she?" asked Maggie, running over to the bedroom door.

"Much, much better," said Janie, pausing outside the door, "The doctor says everything's fine but she still needs to take it easy. You'll be off home this weekend, so you and the twins will see her soon. Are you alright, Maggie darling? You're looking very tired."

"I'm alright Auntie Janie." But Maggie didn't really feel very well at all. Home at the weekend and still five eggs to go!

*****

Nanny Gardner had made one of her wonderful stews full of marvellous and unusual vegetables and they all sat down to eat around the big pine kitchen table. Uncle Charles had baked two granary loaves which tasted miles better than the sort you got from shops.

There was a crack like a snapping branch outside the kitchen window and a yelp of pain. Maggie glanced at the window and thought she saw a shadowy shape disappear around the corner.

"Probably foxes. I spotted them the other night hanging around the house," said Auntie Janie, "We seem to be under siege from wild animals lately don't we? If everyone's finished their first course there'll be popcorn with butterscotch sauce for dessert."

The children all lowered their eyes and stared down at their plates. Maggie felt very proud of them all. They were brilliant at keeping her important secrets.

After all the popcorn and butterscotch had been eaten, the children went out into the garden. Maggie sent Autumn running ahead just in case the spy bikers were hiding somewhere nearby but, although the dog did a great deal of sniffing about, she found nothing.

"Tomorrow," said Maggie to the others, we have to find a way to talk to *Barglor*. We're definitely being watched every day."

*****

The creature that lurked in the murky waters of the forgotten ocean pushed as hard as it could with all four of its powerful legs. With a noise like a mighty cork being pulled from a giant bottle it heaved its massive body off the ocean floor. Sand swirled in clouds around it as it stood on its four long scaly feet, swaying uncertainly as it tried to balance. Great folds of dark blue and purple skin hung from its body, making it look as if it was wearing a huge velvet duvet. A few people living on a small island saw that a brand new island had appeared on their horizon, looking misty, blue and mountainous. Amazed, they went to tell the other islanders. But, when they came back later, the brand new island had completely disappeared under the waves.

*****

Wednesday

Rick had been asked to play his guitar at somebody's birthday lunch in the next town and so he offered to give the children a lift to the river as it was on his way. As they were a bit bored with walking round the village waiting for the next clue to appear, they were quite pleased at the change of scene.

He parked just before a little stone bridge and the children all piled out of the van. Maggie looked up and down the road both ways. No signs of spies.

The river was running very fast over scattered rocks. It looked exactly like frothy milk. Maggie gazed out at it from the bridge.

"There's an old man fishing down there," she said.

"Well we won't see any Egg Keepers with him around," said Holly.

They decided they would stroll through a sweet little riverside wood carpeted with bluebells.

"Let's eat our packed lunch here!" suggested Mike.

They were just finishing the last of Auntie Janie's fruitcake when the silence was broken by a strange, cackling laughing sound.

"Ghosts…" whispered Sid, nudging Colin in the ribs.

"Vampires…" said Colin, winking at Sid.

Emma started to cry.

"Stop it, twins!" said Maggie. "It's nothing to worry about, Emma. It was probably just a fox calling. They can sound really weird sometimes."

Then they heard the eerie laugh again.

"I'd be happier if it *was* a ghost or a vampire," said Mike, "I'm more worried that it's those two biker spies trying to spook us!"

They packed up their stuff and hurried back through the wood. Then, out of the trees right in front of them flew a bright green bird. It soared up and down, laughing and shrieking as it crossed the clearing and disappearing from view as quickly as it had arrived.

"We've been running away from a noisy spooky green woodpecker!" exclaimed Mike.

They all laughed, feeling very relieved indeed.

*****

The creature moved slowly over the ocean floor. As it dragged its great tail along the

110

seabed it left a furrow as deep as the tallest tree is tall. Its clawed feet, like diggers, cut big scoops out of the sand which it then flung out behind. Its head hung nearly to the floor as it moved along. Every fold of its body looked miserable because it was terribly, terribly sad.

*****

The fisherman they had first spotted from the bridge was packing up his gear.

"Hello there, Holly!" he called.

"Hello, Mr. Mugford!" said Holly, "I didn't realise it was you!"

"What's going on around here today?" said Mr. Mugford, "Has a rare bird been sighted or something?"

"Not that I know of," said Holly. "Why?"

"It's usually a quiet spot as you know," said Mr. Mugford,"Today, I haven't had a minute's peace. First some strange old chap roared up on a motorbike, and then two more bikers showed up and had a chat with him – a young couple with binoculars slung round their necks. All three of them birdwatchers I suppose. Now you lot tramping through! I expect they'll come thundering back soon so I'm giving up fishing. I only come here for the peace and quiet. Not much of that to be had today! I might as well go home!"

Holly looked at Dave who looked at Maggie. Maggie raised her eyebrows at Mike. *Professor Falconer is back after us again* she thought, and she could see from the expressions on everyone's faces that they knew it too. They all really wanted to go home and be safe with Nanny Gardner, Auntie Janie and Uncle Charles, but they knew they had to stay outside to have a chance of finding another egg. So they decided to rest by the goat shed at the side of the field and see what happened next. After about half an hour they were just about to give up and go home when Dave suddenly said, "That chaffinch over there is behaving oddly. It keeps turning round to look at me."

"It must be your turn to get the dragon's egg, Dave," said Mike, who was secretly hoping it was his own turn. They all watched the chaffinch. Sure enough, it flew to the stone wall next to Dave and, turning its pretty pink head towards him, it began to sing:

A plump, round orange or a tangerine.
We carve orange pumpkins at Halloween.
Gold fish glow orange in a big glass tank.
Marigolds grow orange on a grassy bank.
You eat orange spaghetti on buttered toast,
Or orange carrots with Sunday roast,
You get orange peaches out of a can,
You bake orange jelly into a flan.

Led to the orange egg by a black crow
There's a cold grey stone with a fiery glow.

When the chaffinch flew away, Dave looked at everyone, his eyes wide with surprise, "Seems we're going to get an orange egg next, guys!"

They decided to follow the path by the small wood because they knew they could just dive behind the tall trees and hide if they heard or saw something. Then they spotted a fishing lake just beyond the hedgerow. It was circular, completely still, and the deepest darkest blue, reflecting the golden pines that surrounded it.

112

"I want to try something…" said Mike. He turned to face the lake, took a deep breath and yelled, "Hello!"

"Hello, hello, hello, hello!" shouted his voice back at him..

"It's a great echo, Mike!" said Dave, "The echo happens, kids, because the lake is round and completely surrounded by tall trees that bounce back the sound over the surface."

Autumn, startled by the noise, started to bark loudly. A stream of barks came straight back to her. She looked round, trying to work out where all the other dogs were. The children all laughed at her. The lake and the trees laughed back at them. It was good to feel free and happy and joyful for a few minutes. It was very tiring being guardians of the special eggs and being chased by weird bikers all the time.

They shouted and shouted and sang and sang. Maggie even played her penny whistle, enjoying how the pretty musical echoes came bouncing back across the surface of the lake. Mike taught the twins how to throw stones and make them bounce across the surface of the water.

"We must all keep looking out for crows, kids," said Maggie. "Don't forget today's clue!"

Just as she said this, a huge black crow with a broad white streak on one wing landed on a tree stump. They all stared at it. The crow started to peck at the stump and it was then that they noticed that the stump was covered with a small bright orange fungus which grew in layers all down one side of it.

"It's fantastic!" gasped Mike. "Like molten lava!"

Dave bent down to take a look at it and as he did this he caught his foot in a tree root and tripped over. The crow didn't seem startled by this. It flew up slowly from the stump and then landed on a small dark rock on the shore of the lake. Mike and the twins helped Dave back to his feet and all the boys went over to the rock together. The base of the rock was covered in bright orange moss.

As Dave bent down to rub his sore ankle, he spotted something glowing on the ground at the foot of the rock. It was the orange egg! He held it up for the others to admire.

There was a tiny little squeak that seemed to come out of nowhere and *Barglor* jumped down on Dave's shoulder, "Good, oh guardians, very, *very* good!" said *Barglor* and was gone before anyone could warn him about the Professor Falconer and his spy biker squad.

*****

Thursday

They all woke up early the next morning and gathered in Holly's room where the orange egg had been placed beside the other two on the window shelf.

"We've *got* to find the Egg Keepers!" said Maggie anxiously, "Half of us are going home at the weekend and we still don't know what we're supposed to do with these dragons' eggs. We never get a chance to talk to *Barglor* properly any more. He doesn't seem to want to stick around us, plus we don't even know where the Rising Place is!"

"I'll ask my Mum if I can help her do us a picnic lunch," said Holly "and then we can return to the mountain and try and find him."

"Yeah," agreed Dave, "It's our best chance of finding out what we still need to know. We know our way round now after all."

"It's bed-room cleaning day today kids! So you'd best clear up a bit before I dust and vacuum!" It was Auntie

Janie's voice, shouting up the stairs. They all stared at Holly's ornament shelf in horror, "And we're popping Autumn down to a friend of mine to get her coat clipped," continued Janie, "Her fur is full of grass burrs and twigs so she stays *here* today please!"

"Bring the dragons' eggs now!" ordered Maggie. "We can't risk leaving them in Holly's room on cleaning day!"

Maggie, Dave and Mike each hid an egg in their rucksacks.

"Look after each other!" called Nanny as they trooped out of the house, "Ring me from the pub phone box if you need a lift home from Rick!"

Just as they reached the gate at the bottom of the garden, a bird flew down to the ground right in front of them, looked around very carefully and then flicked its wing downwards and removed its cloak.

"We need to talk to you urgently, oh guardians!" It was *Chikka*. A creamy cloud of meadow pipit Egg Keepers flew down to join her.

"We need to talk to you too!" said Maggie. "We haven't got a clue what we're supposed to be doing and time is running out fast!"

"We've watched over you every day," said *Chikka*, "You have always got someone close behind you. We never take chances on being seen by the un-chosen. There are three bad ones who follow you."

"Yes, we know," said Maggie.

"Are they around today?" asked Mike.

"Not at this moment," said *Chikka*, "otherwise we would not be here. We don't often leave our meadow home. Usually we send other birds to help you."

"Yes we know other birds have been helping us," said Maggie. "And we're very grateful but…"

"Do you recall *Klaku*, the green woodpecker," interrupted *Chikka*. "He is one of the Chief Egg Keepers. There was much danger that day and so he was sent specially."

"*Please* listen to me, *Chikka*." pleaded Maggie, "We're going home on Sunday and its Thursday already and we're supposed to be saving all seven dragons' eggs, but dangerous people are always watching the house and we think they are even trying to get in through Holly's window. Luckily the Stone Egg's safe in the rainbow cave, and they haven't managed to steal the three dragons' eggs we've got, but they might manage it…"

She stopped because she had run out of breath.

"You're doing very well, Seven Guardians," said *Chikka*, "Our trust in you is well-placed. Yes, there is certain danger all around, even beneath our feet, but we must all have courage."

"Can I ask you something?" insisted Holly. "Why won't you and the Dragon Speakers make it up? You're arguing over something that happened thousands of years ago. I think that's *extremely* silly."

The meadow pipit Egg Keepers turned to Holly with a look of horror and quickly fastened on their bird-cloaks.

"Oh, no!" said Holly. "I'm sorry. I didn't mean to upset you! *Please* don't go!"

Annoyed, The Egg Keepers took off high into the air and disappeared into the sky. *Chikka* gave Maggie a sad and disappointed look as she hovered above her head. Then she vanished too.

"Well, that's just great!" said Dave. "Well done, Holly."

"I'm so sorry everyone," said Holly. "I really didn't mean to make them go."

"It's alright, Holly," said Maggie. "It was a very good question and it would have saved us an awful lot of bother if you had convinced the silly things to just make up their quarrels and stop arguing."

"The post bus stops at the crossroads in about half an hour," said Dave, "if we leave here now we can get a ride all the way home. The whole day is ruined any way."

But he had barely got these words out when an enormous electric blue dragonfly skimmed over the surface of the water and then hovered right over Mike's head.

"It wants something!" said Sid

"Definitely!" said Colin.

"Look!" exclaimed Emma, "it wants us to go back to the edge of the lake."

They followed the dragonfly and watched it as it darted around an overhanging willow tree. A kingfisher was perched on the lowest trailing branch. It bowed at the children and began to sing:

Bluebottle fly and Great Blue Whale,
Bright blue feathers in a peacock's tail.
Blue the mountains far away.
Blue the dragonflies in May.
Blue the colour of a baby's eyes.
Blue the seas and blue the skies.
Darkest blue the sky at night.
Blue the pen you use to write.

To find the egg as blue as sky,
Follow the flight of the dragonfly.

Then the kingfisher shot away over the water and disappeared.

117

"I'm getting the next egg!" shouted Mike, almost losing his balance and toppling into the lake with excitement.

"A blue one!" said Colin, dancing about.

"Hooray!" said Sid.

The blue dragonfly had settled on Mike's arm.

"Off you go then dragonfly!" said Mike. "I'm ready when you are!"

The dragonfly flew along the bank of the lake and, after a little while, it settled on a big round brown stone. Mike crept forward and moved the stone carefully to one side. He picked something up from the little gap underneath it. It was a tiny bright blue egg.

"That makes *four*!" announced Emma proudly.

"Almost one egg for every colour of the rainbow," said Holly. "Just got yellow, indigo and violet left to go!"

They all clustered around Mike to admire the shimmering blue egg then Mike put it carefully into Maggie's rucksack. The twins clapped their hands and grinned.

"Oh, yes, it's all going to be *great*, isn't it?" said Maggie trying hard to sound cheerful. "Soon we'll have seven baby dragons to look after. Life should really calm down then!

"Cheer up, Mags!" said Mike, grinning from ear to ear, "Let's try and catch that post-bus! I'm starving hungry!"

*****

The creature dragged itself along the sea floor. It realised it could feel only pain, the pain of loneliness, the pain of jealousy, the pain of loss.

118

Its insides simply ached with sadness and its tears fell like huge crystal balls bouncing along the soft sand. It felt torn apart by its longing for love. Every step it took was agony.

*****

The white dragon shouted as he kicked the white walls of his castle. "Why am I so angry!? I didn't used to feel like this. Is writing down the poetry making me feel this way? Before the poetry came into my head I didn't know what was going on out there. I thought that this castle, this moon, was all there was left. Now I can see it all in my head. What good is it to have a whole world in my imagination, a world I can't reach, that I will never see?" His howl of sadness sounded like a steam train in a tunnel high up in the snowy mountains.

*****

Friday

The next day dawned and, over breakfast, the children asked the grown-ups once again if they could make the most of playing outside.

"Off into the wilds are we? Bet you thought you'd have your noses stuck in your computer tablets all holidays!" said Uncle Charles, smiling at Maggie and Mike. "Wouldn't have worked though. Broad-band and wi-fi reception is absolute rubbish round here. Give me the great outdoors every time! Enjoy!"

Maggie and Mike exchanged a look.

"*Barglor* didn't turn up when Mike got the egg yesterday," whispered Holly to Maggie as they all trooped out to the tree-house for a meeting.

"It's not your fault at all, Holly," said Maggie. "They are very touchy little things with very little patience."

"Me and Dave had better go and check the bikers' campsite. See what they're up to," said Mike.

"I think we should come with you, boys," said Maggie, "Time's getting short and we all have to stay together for the magic to happen properly."

And so they all carefully made their way to the edge of the field where the bikers had pitched their tent.

"They've gone," said Dave as he stared through his binoculars. "I reckon it's safe to approach."

The only sign that anyone had been camping there was a rectangle of yellowing grass where the tent had been. They looked around them carefully.

Maggie was the first to see it. She screamed. A terrible scene lay before them. The big grey rock was smeared with blood. The ground around the rock was littered with the tiny mangled bodies of bats.

Maggie bent down to look more closely.

"Oh no, no, no! It's the Dragon Speakers!" she cried. "Here's *Barglor*, look!"

She reached down and touched the tiny body. It moved weakly. *Barglor* managed to lift his head a little and started to whisper something to her. She had to lean very close to him to catch what he was saying.

"We had…to defend our cave… from an evil man. He was waiting for us today when we came out. He tried to force his way in. We had to fight. Many of our number have been lost."

He lay back on the ground, exhausted. Maggie wiped the tears from her face.

"Professor Falconer…" hissed Mike under his breath.

"Where is the man now?" Maggie asked gently.

"We drove him away," murmured *Barglor*. "We bit him many, many times but he was very strong." He rested his head on the ground and shut his eyes.

"Oh, *Barglor*," sobbed Holly, kneeling on the ground beside him. "Please, *please* don't die!"

"What can we *do*?" sobbed Emma.

"There is nothing you can do, little guardian," whispered *Barglor*. "We have died defending the Stone Egg. Many others of our kind remain to continue the task."

"Oh, poor *Barglor*…" sniffed the twins, wiping their noses on their hand.

"Can't we do something, anything, to help you live?" persisted Maggie.

"There would have been a way," said *Barglor*, "if… but no, I will not!"

"*Barglor*, you *must* tell me," urged Maggie.

Barglor screwed his eyes shut. "Egg-Keepers…" he just about managed to say it. Maggie picked him up, holding his little body in her hands and ran to the top of the slope, shouting as loudly as she could.

"*Chikka*!" she yelled. "*Chark! Klaku*! Help us! Please help us!"

Her voice echoed around the mountains. The other children stared at her.

"Stop yelling Maggie," said Mike "The bikers might hear you, or that horrible old weirdo!"

"Listen!" cried Sid.

"Birds!" cried Colin.

Sure enough, from way off they heard the noise of hundreds and hundreds of chirping birds. The amazing sound grew louder and louder.

"They heard me!" shouted Maggie above the noise.

A large black cloud was moving towards them, nearer and nearer until it was right overhead. It was the biggest flock of birds any of them had ever seen! They were landing in the trees, on the rocks and on the grass all around the children. Many of them were Egg Keepers and they removed their bird cloaks as they landed.

A red kite soared down to the ground at Maggie's feet. It was an Egg Keeper too, skin rusty red as he threw off his bird-cloak, hair black and curly, wings cream veined with black. He wore a suit of fine pale cloth and long golden boots. On his head was a beautiful golden crown. He swept the children a deep bow.

"I am *Peeeooo*," he said, "First Prince of the Rainbow Mountain. You are The Seven. For what reason did you summon us?"

"Oh, thank you for coming, *Peeeooo*!" said Maggie. "The Dragon Speakers have been attacked, most of them are dead. I know you don't speak to each other but *Barglor* whispered 'Egg-Keepers' to me and so that is why I called for you. We didn't know what else to do!"

Maggie held out her hands towards him. In them she held the lifeless body of *Barglor*.

Peeeooo gazed down at *Barglor*. "We must act quickly," he said and turning to the Egg Keepers and the other birds he announced in a powerful voice, "We must put our disagreements aside. It is time. But I cannot decide this without your consent and support."

The birds and the Egg Keepers stood looking at him for many moments. The children watched them, hardly daring to breathe. Then the Egg Keepers raised their right hands in a salute and all the other birds chirped loudly.

"Thank you, friends!" announced *Peeeooo*. "Now I need the permission of the dragons. That may prove to be more difficult."

He turned and walked towards the grey rock where all the bodies of the Dragon Speakers lay. He faced the rock and started to speak in a strange, warbling language. Suddenly, a small doorway opened in the rock itself. *Peeeooo* turned to the children.

"Please wait here!" he said.

He stepped through the doorway. It closed behind him. The children, the Egg Keepers and the crowd of birds waited. After a short while, the doorway reopened and *Peeeooo* stepped out. He walked solemnly to the centre of the group.

"I have permission!" he said. "But we must hurry!"

Maggie stepped forward. *Peeeooo* walked towards her. Maggie rested *Barglor* on the ground in front of *Peeeooo*. "Only the Earth has power over life and death," he said.

Then he stooped low, picked up a few crumbs of earth and laid them on *Barglor's* chest. He touched *Barglor's* forehead with his slender finger-tips and said a few words in the strange warbling language. Amazed, they saw *Barglor* stir a little, and then sit up.

"No!" cried *Barglor* in alarm when he saw *Peeeooo* standing over him.

"We must talk, *Barglor*," said *Peeeooo*, raising his hand to calm him. "We have many things to say to each other. I have spoken with the dragons." He gently touched *Barglor's* forehead once more and *Barglor* sighed and relaxed.

Then *Peeeooo* signaled to the other Egg Keepers and they started to run from one dead Dragon Speaker to another, sprinkling earth on them, touching them and speaking in the strange language. One by one, slowly but surely, the Dragon Speakers all sat up and looked around them.

"We are grateful to you, Seven Guardians," said *Peeeooo* to the children, "You have made us see how foolish we have all been for such a very long time." Then he bowed down to *Barglor* and *Barglor* bowed in return. The other Egg Keepers all bowed down to the Dragon Speakers who all stood up and bowed to the Egg Keepers.

Barglor flew over to stand beside *Peeeooo*.

"Thank you, Maid Maggie," Barglor said, "Thank you all. But now it is best that you leave this place and return home immediately."

"We'll leave you all to talk amongst yourselves," said Maggie.

The children turned away obediently. Maggie found herself taking one last look over her shoulder before she turned the curve of the hill. Much to her delight, The Egg Keepers and the Dragon Speakers were deep in conversation.

*****

The creature trudged on over miles of deserted seabed. Its feet were heavy with misery and guilt as it thought dark thoughts of abandonment and betrayal. Fish swam away as it approached. Sea creatures hid in crevasses or burrowed beneath the surface of the sandy floor. Everything left it alone.

*****

Chapter 5

Fortune-Tellers and Festivals

"No!" cried Maggie, as they walked home along the village's main street. "Quick!"

Professor Falconer was coming out of the chemist's shop! The children stepped back into the overhanging awning of the greengrocer's shop opposite so that he wouldn't see them.

"He's a mess!" said Mike. "He's covered in plasters, and he's limping!"

"Yeah, looks like the Dragon Speakers really roughed him up!" laughed Dave.

They peered at him as he hobbled away down the road, watching until he was out of sight.

"Serves him right!" said Sid.

"Yeah!" agreed Colin.

"We'd better go in case he comes back," said Holly. "He won't be in a very good mood."

When they got home they found Nanny Gardner getting washing off the clothesline.

"Guess what?" she said. "Rick and I have managed to get a gig playing at a town festival."

"That's great, Nanny," said Holly as they went indoors. "We'll be able to come and watch you!"

Mike, who had gone ahead of them into the house, gave a loud yell and they all rushed in to find him pointing at the television.

Professor Falconer's face looked back at them from the screen.

"Good gracious!" Nanny exclaimed. "Isn't that the horrible man who was bothering Maggie at the Easter Egg hunt? What on earth has he been up to now?!"

The image of the scowling Professor faded into the next news item. "What was it saying about him, Janie?"asked Uncle Charles.

"He claims he was attacked by vampire bats on a mountain," said Auntie Janie. "It's a ridiculous thing to say. Our local bats are sweet little creatures."

"He was probably up to no good again," said Nanny Gardner, shuddering. "Nasty peculiar man."

"They're going to investigate his claim, "said Uncle Charles. "They have to find the cave to be on the safe side. Bat bites can be poisonous sometimes."

"They won't find it," said Mike.

Maggie frowned at him to keep him quiet.

"He deserved to be bitten," said Sid.

"Yeah," said Colin, "He shouldn't have gone poking around…"

*****

Rick had just driven off in the van to see the people who were organizing the music festival when Nanny Gardner gathered all the children together. She insisted that the children help her in the kitchen as it was such a wet and blustery afternoon. They had no choice but to try and enjoy helping her make batches of pies and cakes but, although it was always fun helping Nanny cook, inside they were incredibly worried about being able to find the next dragon's egg while there was still time. It was late afternoon before the rain eased sufficiently for them to take Autumn for her afternoon walk.

This time they decided to walk across the village green to the rain-swollen river and eventually found themselves peering in through the windows of the old, derelict watermill.

"Look," said Holly. "Some-one's been sleeping in there. They've made a bed out of bracken with an old blanket on top."

"There's a load of empty beer cans too," said Maggie, "and fish and chip wrappers, and sticking plaster boxes."

They all looked at one another, "Professor Falconer!" they all said together.

"Let's get out of here," said Mike. "He may still be around."

"Maggie…" hissed Emma. "There's a big bird looking at me in a funny way. It's got a white collar, like a vicar, and its chest is sort of violet."

Can't be another egg in one day, thought Maggie. *Unless Barglor has finally realised that our time is running out.*

The woodpigeon was staring hard at Emma. It began to sing in a gentle, cooing voice:

Violets with their faint sweet smell.
Violet mother of pearl in a shell.
Violet skin of a wood-mouse's ear.
Young birds before their feathers appear.
Violet the light from an amethyst glows
Like mist on the moor where heather grows.
Like silver fish with their violet gills,
Violet the shadows on snowy hills.

The violet egg is in island mist.
It rests by the well where the lovers kissed.

The woodpigeon stopped singing, spread its wings and flew off.

"Let's get a move on. Professor Weirdo could come back at any time!" said Mike.

"I'm getting a violet egg," said Emma happily as they ran away from the old water mill. "That big bird just sang to me." She skipped on ahead along the path.

"Where are you going, Emma!" called Maggie. "I'm not sure they'd let us find a second egg on the same day!"

"*Barglor* can count, can't he?" said Dave. "He must know we're back at school in three days. There's an island on other side of the old water mill."

They all followed Dave across a row of stepping stones. The warm sun was heating up the wet grass and strands of creamy mist rose up like bonfire smoke.

"I've found the little well!" cried Emma, "Look, over where the misty bit is - just like the clue said!"

They gazed at the tiny well with its pretty yellow stone walls and gnarled wooden roof.

"How sweet," said Holly.

"Wishing-Well," said Maggie, reading the old, faded sign. "Make a wish and your true love will appear."

Emma was scrabbling in the grass at the base of the well.

"Mind out, Emma,"warned Maggie. "Be very careful."

"Found it!" Emma said, ignoring Maggie. She held up a gleaming violet egg. "Oh wow! I really got one!"

Her excited voice sent a flock of birds squawking into the air just as *Barglor* landed on her shoulder.

"Good to see you well again, *Barglor*," said Maggie, "And thank you for letting us find two eggs today."

Barglor smiled at her sweetly, "A reward for my life, Maid Maggie." And he flew away without another word.

*****

Saturday

"We've got that festival gig today, kids," said Nanny
Gardner as they gathered round the breakfast table, "It's
quite a distance away so we'll need to take a picnic.
Auntie Janie and Uncle Charles are staying here so it's
best that Autumn stays with them. The noise of the
music and crowds might all be a bit too much for her."

"Just let's go with them," said Maggie to reassure the
others when they had gathered at the tree-house for
their meeting,"The Egg-Keepers and *Barglor* always
manage to find us. We'll be fine wherever we are."

After they had piled all the musical instruments into
Nanny Gardner's car and Rick's van, they all set out on
their journey across the misty mauve mountains.

After an hour's drive, they arrived at the festival
which was taking place in a very pretty old town
square. There were crowds of people everywhere
strolling by or browsing the colourful stalls. No matter
where the children looked there were tempting things
for sale. Among the crowd wandered jugglers and fire-
eaters and there were people in funny costumes on high
stilts selling balloons.

"Now you older boys make sure no-one gets into
trouble," Nanny Gardner called as she and Rick set up
their musical instruments on the stage. "Go and have
yourselves a fabulous, fun time and meet me back by
the main stage in one hour's time!"

"Can we go and watch the fire-eaters?" asked Sid.

"I'm going to follow the stilt-walkers!" said Colin.

"Can we go to see the fortune-teller?" asked Emma.

"Tell you what, I'll take care of the lads and you girls do your own thing. We'll all meet back here in half an hour," Dave said.

Maggie, Holly and Emma walked over to the fortune-teller's tent and entered through the bright, colourful bead curtain. It was quite gloomy inside and they could only just see a very small woman sitting behind a table near the back.

"Hello, my dears," she said. "Come and sit down next to me. What do you want to know?"

The tent was warm and smelled like Christmas trees, treacle toffee and cinnamon all mixed up. The fortune teller wore flowing green robes embroidered with silver dragonflies and she had a string of silver coins across her forehead. Huge silver rings decorated her hands. The woman gave Maggie a twinkling smile.

"How much is it, please?" Maggie said, wondering if the woman could really see into the future.

"Fifty pence each, my dear," said the woman. "You can pay me when we're done. Give me your hand, child," and she reached out and took hold of Maggie's hand.

Then she jumped and stared intently into Maggie's eyes. "I was hoping you'd appear today, my dear," she said. "I saw it in the crystal ball. I've always seen visions. So did my mother before me and her mother before her too."

"What do you mean?" asked Maggie, trying to pull her hand away from the woman's grasp. The fortune teller's dark blue eyes flashed from beneath her fringe of silvery curls.

"Now, don't be frightened, child," said the woman kindly. "I mean you no harm. You are just as I saw you in my dream. You are a child of great courage and you have been chosen to protect something very precious.

But you must be on your guard. And as for you, little one," she said to Emma, who was staring at the woman open-mouthed, "you must be careful too. Help your cousin all you can. She touched Emma's cheek lightly with her finger tips.

"And you, my dear," she said, turning to Holly, who had stood up from her chair and was looking a little nervous, "you will find what you seek in the Milky Way."

"Who *are* you?" asked Maggie. "How do you know all this?" *And how does she know Emma and I are cousins?* she thought.

"I am your friend, my dears, and I wish you all good fortune. The silent voices cannot harm you, but make sure you listen to your dreams."

"What?" said Maggie, thinking, *How on earth does she know about the voices in the cave?*

"What voices?" asked Holly, "…and what's the milky-way?"

"I will see you all again very soon," the woman said. "We have much to talk about in the future. Goodbye."

The fortune teller walked to the doorway of her tent and held the curtain open for them. The three girls didn't know what else to say. As they walked past her she pressed something into their hands, gave each of them a gentle little push, and suddenly they were outside, blinking in the bright sunlight.

Maggie said, "We didn't pay her."

"Look what she gave me," said Holly holding out a ring made of plaited silver and set with a stone of very deep blue. The stone had tiny flecks of gold in it.

"That's pretty," said Maggie. She looked down at her own hand. She was holding a tiny golden bird on a chain.

"It's a Golden Eagle!" she exclaimed. "What have you got, Emma?"

"Oooh!" Emma said, holding out a fine gold necklace set with tiny mauve stones. "They're exactly the same colour as my dragon's egg!"

"They look like amethysts," said Maggie. "My Mum's got a bracelet like that. The fortune teller seemed to know a lot about us."

"Perhaps we should have asked her more questions," said Holly.

"What was all that about silent voices?" asked Emma.

"Nothing," said Maggie. "Don't worry about that. I still think we'd better go back and pay her. It's only fair."

And so they turned to go back.

"Oh!" Holly exclaimed in surprise.

Men were busy loading the fortune-teller's tent onto a lorry. A hand-written sign had been put up. It read: ***Madam Verity has been called away***. Of the mysterious little woman, there was no sign.

*****

The three girls found Mike and Dave watching some banjo players on the stage.

"Where on earth are the twins?" Maggie demanded. "You were supposed to watch them!"

Mike and Dave turned round in surprise. "I told them to stick with us, Maggie," said Dave. "They must have sneaked off when we turned our backs!"

They all ran round the festival stalls in a bit of a panic, calling out "Sid" and "Colin" at the tops of their voices.

"There they are!" cried Holly.

Sid and Colin were wandering towards them.

"Where have you *been*?" demanded Maggie.

"Oh, hello," said Colin. "We've just been chatting to a nice little lady."

"Yes," said Sid, "she said that we had two of the seven."

"What?" exclaimed Maggie.

"And then she said, 'When one is taken from seven, one is divided by two,' or I think that's what she said, I didn't really understand her," said Colin, frowning as he tried to remember.

"And she said to beware of the falcon," added Sid.

"Then she gave us these," said Colin, showing them a key ring which held a tiny green dragon made out of some sort of crystal. Sid held out another key-ring exactly like Colin's, but red in colour.

"They fit together, look!" said Sid. "She showed us how."

He put the little green dragon against the red one that Colin held, nose to tail, and twisted it slightly. They fitted together perfectly like pieces of a jigsaw.

"Oh!" said Holly. "Look! They make an egg shape!"

"This woman, did she have crazy curly hair and blue eyes?" said Dave.

"Yes!" said the twins.

"You saw her too?" exclaimed Maggie.

"Yes, she came up to us at the music stage," said Mike. "She was selling bunches of heather to people. She gave me this." He held out a chunky silver ring with a clear blue stone set in the centre.

"And she gave me this," said Dave, showing them a copper ring set with an amber stone.

"She seemed to know us," said Mike.

"Look!" yelled Colin, "Nanny and Rick are starting to sing!"

"I'll bet they'll be the best singers here all day!" said Sid.

*****

*****

"I never see colours," said the white dragon out loud, "unless you count shades of sparkling silver starlight, or planet-light. Mars is reddish silver, and Venus is greenish silver, but everything I can see is mostly black or white, or silver and gold. I wonder if the creatures who see in all the colours of the rainbow could understand how many different shades of white and black there are and, of course, let's not forget about grey. Think how colourless my life would be if it wasn't for dear old grey!" And he began to laugh his hollow cracked laugh, rocking to and fro in his chair, beating his fists on the table until the dust floated around him

134

like mist over a moor. "Grey!" he cackled. "Where would I be without grey?" And he wrote…

Ancient Greece

An astronomer in ancient Greece
Who lived one thousand years B.C.
Did not wake up in time to see
but stayed in bed and missed the scene.

The earth, recovered from her pain,
Had given birth to life again.
But those dragons that remained
Had never guessed
The crime of one, forgotten by the rest.
What would that man have said if he had
viewed an egg become a world before his eyes?
What great mythology there might have been
If he had seen a million dragons rise.
Would some great new religion have been born
If he had looked into the sky that dawn?

*****

No birds or Egg Keepers had found them at the festival and so the children assumed that the Fortune Teller was deeply involved with their quest that day. They were all tired from their long day out, but after tea that evening when the grown-ups were dozing in front of the wood-burning stove, they decided they had better hold a very quick meeting by the goat-shed in the field.

"Oh, look at that poor Magpie on the fence post," said Holly as they all huddled together behind the shed. "It's been soaked by a rain shower. It's sitting fluffing up its wet feathers to get dry again. Now it's staring right at me."

The Magpie stood up on its branch, coughed, and began to sing:

Indigo blackcurrant juice
Indigo blackberry mousse.
Indigo sky encircles the moon.

Indigo irises bloom in June.
The indigo shine of a Magpie's feather.
An indigo cloud in stormy weather.
Indigo Peacock Butterflies.
Indigo Persian kittens' eyes.

The egg is indigo today.
You'll find it in the Milky Way

"Oh, how lovely," said Holly. "It's all joining up like a puzzle! That's what that tent lady at the fair said. But what exactly is the Milky Way, Mr Magpie?"

But the Magpie simply bowed and flew away.

"My turn tonight, my turn tonight!" chanted Holly, "I'm getting an egg, a beautiful indigo egg!"

"Let's get up to the rock quickly!" urged Maggie. "It'll be raining again soon and it's almost twilight!"

The children were very tired indeed by the time reached the top of the mountain that was really a hill. The flat ground around the rock was one huge puddle from heavy showers earlier that day.

"I hope the cave isn't getting flooded," said Maggie.

The twins jumped into the puddle.

"Stop it, twins!" shouted Emma, "That went all over me!"

"Look at the way you can see the sky in the puddle," said Dave. "It's deep blue, like Holly's ring with the gold speckles. And see how the stars that are just beginning to appear in the sky are now reflected in the puddle?"

They all looking up at the darkening sky. Sure enough, tiny pin-pricks of starlight were starting to form in the sky and in the puddle too.

"A dragon's egg as indigo as the night sky..." whispered Maggie.

Holly bent down and trailed her fingers through the puddle dreamily.

"I can identify that carpet of stars," said Dave. "I think you'll find it's the Milky Way, Holly!"

"Thank you, Brain-box brother!" said Holly. "Oh! I *found* it!" She picked up a tiny indigo egg from the very centre of the puddle.

"Good evening," said *Barglor*, suddenly settling on Holly's shoulder, "Only one egg left now to find, dear guardians." And he darted away again into the night.

"Thanks, *Barglor*!" called out Holly happily watching as he flitted over the tops of the trees.

"That means its Maggie's turn next," said Colin.

"And the egg will be yellow," said Sid.

"That means we will have all the colours of the rainbow complete - red, orange, yellow, green, blue, indigo and violet," said Emma.

"How lovely," said Holly. "A rainbow made of eggs!"

"Me, Maggie and Emma are supposed to be going home tomorrow," said Mike. "I hope we can get back up here in time."

"Thanks for reminding me of that," said Maggie gloomily.

They put Holly's egg safely in her rucksack and trudged back down the mountain path to home.

*****

Later that evening, just as the three girls were getting ready for bed, there was a loud knock at the door of Holly's room. Maggie, Holly and Emma instantly looked over at the row of six gleaming eggs hidden amongst the ornaments on Holly's shelf, hoping they would not be noticed. Nanny Gardner walked in.

138

"I've made you girls some hot chocolate with sprinkles," said Nanny putting the tray down on the dressing-table, "Oh, that's such a pretty shelf of ornaments!" she said. "Where did you get all these lovely things, Holly? Look, girls, I wanted you all to see this lovely little tapestry picture. I bought it at the festival from an antiques stall. It only cost 50 pence – what a bargain! Something drew me to it and I just had to have it!"

The girls were happy to look at it as it meant Nanny would concentrate on the tapestry rather than the eggs. They bent their heads over to study it carefully – and then they all looked at one another in shock and surprise.

"It's a Victorian sampler," said Nanny Gardner, "Such beautiful stitching isn't it? In the old days, little girls used to make them to practice their needlework. See the sweet little chapel here at the bottom with a rainbow over it, and lots of birds, or are they bats do you think? And is that a tiny dragon? I think it might be. Let's read the poem shall we...."

Maggie looked at Holly and Emma and gulped. Their eyes could not have been wider with surprise.

"Do you want to read it, Maggie?" said Nanny. "Go ahead..."

And so Maggie started to read...

I am a child of the rainbow.
I was born in a storm
When the sun and rain lived life together.
I am a creature of light.
I am made of bright colours
Which fade or glow bright in foul or fair weather.
When the sun glows deep orange
In skies of dark blue

When heavy black thunderclouds form.
When I see silver flashes
And hear the sky roar
I go out and run through the storm.
Down soft violet hillsides
Streams run rusty red.
Green trees are washed clean by the rain.
Where golden sun breaks
Through the indigo clouds
I can dance in the rainbow again.

And Maggie felt a shiver run down her spine. There had been another little girl, over one hundred years ago, who had dreamed the same dreams. Had she been a chosen one too? Had she succeeded or failed?

"Very well read, darling," Nanny Gardner said. "This makes me think of you so strongly and so I want to give it to you. Think of it as a slightly early birthday present. You were born on a stormy night, you know. Oh, and by the way, girls, I bumped into one of my oldest friends today at the festival! We went to school together. Haven't seen her for years! She was like the sister I never had. She always looked after me when I needed help. She makes the most wonderful rings and necklaces and she tells people's fortunes too! Wasn't that a strange coincidence? Sometimes we find ourselves in exactly the right place at exactly the right time!"

*****

The white dragon wiped the ink from his claw, heaved himself to his feet and carried the large, heavy book of poems over to a shelf. As he walked he disturbed a cloud of white dust which rose around him like smoke.

140

His throat creaked into action. "How I'd love to see a real rainbow!" he said. "In my mind I only see dream rainbows."

*****

Sunday

"We're all going out for our final morning walk together!" called Maggie.

"Don't be late for lunch!" called Auntie Janie. "Ring us from the phone box by the pub if you need a lift home. You've got a long journey home this afternoon, don't forget!"

"I'd forgotten all about school," said Holly gloomily.

"Yeah…nightmare…" chorused the twins.

Maggie felt desperate but was trying hard to hide it from the others. After all, she was the one who had been chosen to sort everything out and she couldn't imagine what she had to do next now that six eggs were safe. In fact, with every dragon's egg they collected, she had grown more and more anxious. Time was ticking away fast. Nanny Gardner and Rick were due to drive them home straight after lunch!

"We could run away," suggested Colin, once they were out of Nanny Gardner's earshot.

"We could hide in the mountains until after the Stone Egg has risen," said Sid.

"When we came back they'd be so pleased to see us, they wouldn't be cross," said Emma.

"Those are good ideas, kids, but not really very practical," said Maggie.

"I don't see that there's anything we *can* do," said Dave as they crossed the goats' field.

141

"We'll just have to wait and see," said Holly. "Where shall we go today?"

"I think we should walk over to the Rainbow Mountain," said Mike, "to see what's beyond the rock and the woods." He gazed at the narrow ridge that ran along the top of the mountain.

"Hey! I thought I saw a man over there!" hissed Emma.

She pointed at something but no-one else could spot anything.

"We still need to keep our eyes peeled for Professor Falconer and his two mates," warned Dave.

"I'm sure I did see someone out of the corner of my eye," said Emma.

"We've got Autumn with us," said Maggie. "She'll warn us."

They scrabbled over the loose stones all the way up to the ridge and found themselves looking down at a grassy slope. The other mountains stretched out before them in shades of yellow, orange and violet set against the dark green forests that climbed up their sides. Moving cloud shadows drifted dreamily across the landscape and a red kite soared high in the blue sky. Distant lakes glistened like jewels, streams sparkled like silver ribbons and waterfalls tumbled down as white foam into indigo pools around which creamy fleeced sheep grazed. Tiny villages nestled in the valley far below.

Suddenly Emma shrieked in surprise. She pointed to the far side of the grassy slopes. They all gazed down at what looked like a group of very still, grey, hooded statues.

"It's a stone circle!" exclaimed Maggie.

"I didn't know that was here!" said Holly.

142

"I can't believe we have never found that before!" agreed Dave. "Amazing!"

The stones were dark grey and smooth. The children walked into the very centre of the circle.

"It's like standing inside a bubble of peacefulness," said Holly.

"The grass inside is much thicker and greener than the grass outside," whispered Emma.

"It must have been built thousands of years ago," said Dave. "Just think how hard it must have been to drag these stones all the way up here!"

"It's wonderful," said Maggie. "They told us we would know it when we saw it. This must be The Rising Place! We've actually found it!"

"If the last egg's going to rise from anywhere around here, this would be a great place to let it," agreed Mike.

"Let's stand all round the circle," said Maggie, "one of us in front of each of the seven stones."

"Look," said Holly as they moved round. "The stones look like a bit like us!"

She was right. Maggie and Mike stood in front of two tall, narrow stones, Holly and Dave were standing in front of two shorter, wider stones, Emma chose a much smaller stone, and the twins chose the two jagged stones that looked like one stone split in two. *It's as if the stones chose us* thought Maggie.

"Autumn hasn't got a stone," said Sid.

But Autumn seemed very happy just to lie down in the middle of the circle. She put her head on her paws and went fast asleep.

"Are you okay, Maggie?" said Holly.

"Fine," said Maggie. "A bit tired suddenly." She closed her eyes. "I suppose we just stay here and wait," she said.

"It's very warm and relaxing in here," said Dave sleepily and sat down.

"Mmmm, it's because it's so lovely and sunny," said Emma, yawning widely.

In a few seconds they were all seated on the short grass, snoozing with their backs against their stones.

Maggie dreamed she was going along a crystal-lined tunnel. It was so peaceful that she wouldn't have minded staying there forever. Then she was suddenly out of the tunnel and floating through a fresh and perfumed mist which was changing colour as she flew through its violet, indigo, and blue shades. *I'm flying through a rainbow,* she thought. The mist turned from green to yellow, then to orange. *When the mist turns red,* Maggie thought, *will I hit the ground?* It seemed as if she was whizzing backwards very fast through the world, or perhaps the world was flying forwards past her? She saw cities full of people and strange places. Sometimes, in the crowds of people in the cities, she caught glimpses of girls that looked exactly like her - many different Maggies - who stared back at her. The cities became smaller and the people fewer. Gradually the cities disappeared completely and were replaced by small villages and huge areas of grassland and forests. Finally, she arrived at a place where there were no people at all. She was standing in a grassy meadow in the middle of the stone circle. The very same stone circle. Around her were animals of all kinds wandering about eating the grass, or chasing each other playfully in the sunshine. Birds were singing, beautiful flowers bloomed and insects buzzed around her. Then Maggie saw someone walking towards her. It was herself!

"You're *me!*" she said to the girl. The girl laughed and took hold of Maggie's hand.

Then the meadow faded away and Maggie was flying rapidly back through the villages, the towns, the cities, finally finding herself sitting in the stone circle with the all the others.

She opened her eyes, really not sure what she was going to see. Had the little dream girl who had laughed and held her hand been the little Victorian girl who had sewn the tapestry sampler? Was there really a line of little girls who looked just like her stretching back and back and back in time?

"Wow!" said Mike, opening his eyes. "I've just had this amazing dream!"

"So have I!" shouted Sid. "I went back in time and met myself in a meadow!"

"So did I!" said Holly. "And then I flew through a rainbow!"

"I saw lots of places with me living in them!" shouted Colin.

"And I travelled along a sparkly tunnel!" said Emma, "and went to a place with lots of animals in it."

"There was another me," said Dave in a very serious voice. "He was my friend. It was like another universe or something."

"We've all had exactly the same time-travelling dream!" exclaimed Maggie. "We've gone backwards to show us something important." She stood up and stretched. "I feel wonderful!" she said. "Oh, look up there everyone!"

Wheeling high above their heads was a huge bird.

"What's that?" said Mike. "It's massive!"

"It looks like a golden eagle," said Dave, "but I didn't think that there were any in Wales. They're far rarer than Red Kites."

The huge bird swooped down and landed right in the middle of the stone circle beside Autumn. The children pressed themselves back against the stones in wonder.

The golden eagle reached up with his wing tip, removing his bird cloak and transforming into an Egg Keeper. He was much larger than any of the other Egg Keepers and Autumn whimpered a little. Everything about him was golden - his skin, his hair, his eyes, even his clothes were yellow silk and richly embroidered with delicate strands of gold thread. On his feet were honey-coloured suede bird-foot boots and on his head a fine gold crown. He swept Maggie a low bow.

"Hah!" he exclaimed, "I am *Keesoo*, Most High King of the Whats-its, Ultimate ruler of the Thingummy-Jig. But you can call me Goldie."

He grinned at the children, showing gleaming white teeth.

"Er…hello, King *Keesoo*," said Maggie. "I don't think I can call you Goldie. It doesn't seem very respectful."

"*Keesoo* will do for now, then," the golden man said. "Pleased to meet you."

"What did you say that you were Most High King of?" asked Maggie, "and all the rest of it? I didn't catch it."

"Alright I'll tell you properly," laughed *Keesoo*. "My full title is *Keesoo*, Most High King of the Egg Keepers, Ultimate Ruler of the Skies, First Guardian of the Day. Bit of a mouthful really so I don't tend to say it much."

"Wow!" said Colin.

"I'd tell *everyone* if I had a title like that," said Sid.

"It's only when one doesn't *feel* important that one needs to make oneself *more* so," said *Keesoo*. "I did not choose my titles but I do my best to live up to them."

146

"*Feeling* that you have value is the most important thing whether you have a title or not," he added with a smile.

"Is this the Rising Place please?" said Maggie. "We were just sitting here hoping it was but we fell asleep."

"Yes. And a very powerful place it is," said *Keesoo*.

"We thought it probably was," said Mike.

"I wanted you all to experience its magic," said *Keesoo*. "But a warning. There was danger present a little while ago. A stranger was here."

"So there *was* someone hanging about," said Emma, "I thought so."

"Have they gone now?" asked Maggie nervously.

"For now, we are all safe," said *Keesoo*. "He did not find what he sought. But you must be very careful. The crystal cave has been threatened."

"Yes, we know!" said Maggie. "And the Dragon Speakers were attacked!"

"*Barglor* told me this," said *Keesoo*. "It is wonderful to be able to say that I spoke with *Barglor* after these many years of conflict. We all owe you so much."

"We're just glad we could help," said Maggie.

"The Stone Egg is still in danger," *Keesoo* continued. "An attempt has been made by other forces to flood the cave, but we managed to seal the doorways. Also, attempts have been made to steal the eggs from your home. However, soon you will have all seven of the dragons' eggs in your keeping and so the danger from subterranean enemies will have been averted. We shall meet again at The Rising. I have much to do."

"What's sub-trainian?" asked Colin.

"Underground stuff," replied Sid.

"Mike, Emma, me and the twins have to leave after lunch!" exclaimed Maggie. "Can you *please* tell us what we're supposed to do?"

"You will discover what to do," said *Keesoo*, winking at Maggie. "You'll sort it out, Maid Maggie, for you are of The Line." He flicked his cloak around his shoulders, becoming a Golden Eagle once more.

"Of the Line?" said Maggie, "*please* explain what you mean!" But *Keesoo* had already leapt into the air.

"Trust the Golden Eagle," he called as he soared off the edge of the mountain. "It will protect you!"

"What did he mean?" said Maggie. "He said I was of the line. *What* line? I told him we have to go today! Why won't they *listen* to me?!"

"The Legend says you are descended from Greenwoods, to Gardner and to Rose," said Dave thoughtfully. "Maybe that's the sort of line he means."

"I don't know much about our ancestors," said Maggie.

"We'll have to ask Nanny," said Maggie. "We've got no choice."

But just as the children were preparing to leave the circle, a willow warbler landed on the top of Maggie's stone, fluffed up its yellow feathers and chirped its song:

Up in the sky is the yellow sun
As yellow as butter on a hot cross bun.
At Easter time, yellow chicks hatch
As yellow as flames when you strike a match.
Lemon meringue pie with custard.
Golden egg yolks, yellow mustard.
Golden daffodils in the Spring.
Yellow gold in a wedding ring.

The egg today is gleaming gold.
Prepare for weather wet and cold.

"Thank heavens!" said Maggie, "I'm going to get my yellow egg at last!"

A cloud of golden dragonflies whizzed past her head and landed on a tuft of tall, yellowing grass. She carefully parted the spindly stalks at the base of the tuft.

"I should try and trust our new friends more," she said, holding up a tiny, beautiful golden egg. It shone in her hand like a small sun.

*****

"I can't believe we're back at school tomorrow," said Mike as they walked home. "The holiday's gone so fast!"

"We've done the best we can," said Maggie. "We got the Stone Egg back where it belongs, we've got the Egg Keepers and the Dragon Speakers talking to each other, and we've saved *Barglor* and the others from Professor Weirdo Falconer."

"We've collected the dragons' eggs too, don't forget!" said Emma.

"I don't know what more I can do..." said Maggie, "...we'll just have to leave the dragons' eggs with you." Maggie was looking straight at Dave and Holly, "I do hope you'll be able to get the seven eggs to the Rising Place safely once we've gone - before you have to go back to school yourselves. I trust you both completely you know." Dave and Holly nodded and smiled at her.

"*Barglor* didn't even come to say goodbye to me," added Maggie sadly.

"Even when you found the yellow egg," said Colin.

"I hope the Dragon Speakers are okay," said Sid.

Chapter 6

Walks and Waterfalls

"Life can't exist without water, but I'm here," said the white dragon. "The poor little moon is dead, dry and silent. Am I alive? Is this a life?"

"What must it feel like to be a mountain-dragon on a living world? It must be wonderful to feel the trees growing on your back and to be able to talk to the other mountain dragons. Without water, I can't even cry!"
He lay down full length on the dusty ground. "I would have been a beautiful mountain," he said. "But this won't do. I have important work to finish. I can feel another verse forming in my head."

And he wrote…

Bethlehem

A lonely shepherd saw while watching sheep
A star above a stable by an inn.
He saw the newborn baby there within
Lying in a manger - fast asleep.
What was it that the shepherd saw that night?
That all those people gathered there could see?
A star perhaps - or meteor was there?
A rising world reflecting the sun's glare?
Three Kings followed light trails to the stable.
Draw your own conclusions, if you're able.
But each time that a new Stone Egg appears,
A new time starts that lasts ten thousand years.

*****

"Your Dad just left a message, Maggie," said Nanny Gardner when the children walked into the kitchen.

"Is Mum okay? Is it about the baby? " asked Maggie anxiously.

"Yes, darling, she's absolutely fine and the baby too. Baby's expected any time now," said Nanny Gardner, "but we can stay up here a little bit longer. There was a big electric storm back home and what they call a flash-flood. Your house is alright, and yours too Mike, but your school got it quite badly and needs to dry out. They told your Dad that it will re-open on Wednesday."

Maggie stared at Mike. Two extra days right out of the blue! It was marvellous! A kind of miracle!

"We've been in touch with your Mum and Dad, mate," said Uncle Charles to Mike, "Because of the school flood, they've asked if you and Emma can stay on too. Okay with everyone!"

"Yeah, yeah, yeah!" said Mike, delighted, and Emma did a happy little dance on the spot.

"You lucky lot…" said Dave, and winked at Maggie.

Holly rushed over to Maggie and hugged her. The twins grinned at her and nudged each other.

Maggie found herself so relieved at this wonderful news that she almost started to cry. She blinked back her tears as best she could and turned her head away from the others.

At least I can stop worrying about The Rising quite so much, she thought, *and more importantly, Mum's okay again.*

*****

"Nanny," said Maggie, when they were all sitting round the wood-burning stove that evening, "Will you please tell us about our ancestors. We were all chatting today and realised that we don't know much about them."

"Well, now…" began Nanny Gardner, settling herself more comfortably in her armchair. "Who shall I tell you about first?"

"What did they look like, Nanny? Did they all have fair hair and green eye and freckles like us?" asked Emma.

"Well, my family all have silvery fair curls - my Mum and her Mum and her Mum before her," said Nanny Gardner, "Ash-blonde, my Mum used to call it. And those greeny-brown hazel eyes that you and your cousins have come from the Greenwood side. You ought to ask your Granddad Greenwood who lives in Australia about his family. He had some *very* interesting ancestors, especially his own Great-Great Granddad who kept *enormous* lizards as pets."

Maggie looked at Mike and knew he was thinking the same thing. First dragons, now giant lizards! What an interesting family they had been born into!

*****

The creature on the seabed struggled to keep going. It felt that its body was getting heavier and heavier, as if it were carrying the ocean on its back. It stumbled and then stood still. Its head hung so low that its chin, as prickly as a hedgehog, scraped lines in the fine sand.

*****

Monday.

The waterfall hit the pool in a cloud of white foam.
The sides of the pool were edged with luscious ferns
hanging like green feathers, washed fresh and clean by
the spray that splashed over black rocks worn satin-
smooth by centuries of water. Behind the waterfall was
a cave in which they could glimpse yet more ferns
growing on glistening black walls. Dragonflies soared
over the pool.

Nanny Gardner and Rick had taken Maggie, Emma,
Mike and the twins out for the afternoon and Nanny had
discovered the most glorious place to sit down and rest.
It was a shame not to have Dave and Holly around, but
they would be back from school by 3.45 and so there
would be plenty of time to catch up.

"Can you amuse yourselves for a while?" Nanny said.
"Rick and I are going to sit under this rowan tree and
try and compose some new songs for our show. There
are plenty of places where you can play, but be careful
around the waterfall and the river. The rain from
yesterday has made it very turbulent."

"What's turb-you-lent?" asked Colin

"Dunno." replied Sid.

"It's when the water swirls around very strongly,"
said Emma.

Autumn yawned, rested her head on Nanny Gardner's
lap and closed her eyes.

The children didn't have to be told twice. They were
all eager to continue their adventure. They had shared
out the seven eggs and put them in their rucksacks.
They were ready for anything.

"Now the Seven Guardians have found the seven
eggs, all the other dragons' eggs are supposed to be laid

154

today," said Emma, skipping along the path in excitement. "I wonder if we'll get to see any of them!"

"I've got my binoculars ready!" said Sid, holding them up to his eyes.

I'm not going to let anything bother me today," Maggie thought. "*We're still here, we're still together, and I'm going to try and relax.*"

The path took them right up the hillside until they were edging along the side of a steep cliff which looked down on the river some distance below. Maggie was really starting to enjoy herself.

"Hold on to the trees at the side, kids," said Mike, "you're quite safe if you don't go too near the edge."

Sid and Colin were a little way ahead along a bend in the path when the others heard Colin yell.

"Help!!" he was shouting, "Help! Help!"

"Professor Falconer's down here!!" shouted Sid.

"Sit down, stay where you are and *don't move*!" said Mike to Emma. He and Maggie dashed down the path to find the twins.

Sure enough, facing them was Professor Falconer, a wild look in his eyes, his hands gripping Sid on one side and Colin on the other. The Professor stood on the very edge of the narrow cliff path. Far below, the waterfall crashed over huge rocks and the swollen river cut a curve around an enormous boulder, forming a deep swirling pool.

"Let go of them *now*!" yelled Mike.

"What's the matter with you?" shouted Maggie. "Why can't you leave us *alone*? What do you *want*?"

"You know very well what I want," Professor Falconer said, in a low, sinister voice. "Where's that Stone Egg? I've chased you all over the country, Miss Maggie Gardner, I've watched you walk through solid rock into mountains, I've been arrested, I've been attacked by vampire bats, I've spent a small fortune hiring a couple of losers to help me who turned out to be a waste of space, I've had hardly any sleep for days on end and suffered the most terrible nightmares. It's The Voice from the Deep! Don't you understand?! The Voice from the Deep! He, that *creature*, keeps telling me he needs the Stone Egg. HE WOULD LEAVE ME ALONE AND I COULD GO HOME AND SLEEP IN PEACE IF YOU WOULD JUST GIVE ME THAT BLESSED STONE EGG!!!" His own voice had risen to such a loud pitch that the children trembled. Then Professor Falconer lifted his arms up so high that Sid and Colin's feet dangled in the air.

"I'm losing my patience, Maid Maggie," he hissed through clenched teeth. "Tell me what you've done with the Stone Egg or these lads may have a little accident." He took a step closer to the cliff edge.

"We haven't got it!" said Maggie. "We lost it! Please let them go!" She put her rucksack down on the ground.

"What's in that rucksack?" snapped the Professor. He had loosened his grip on Sid's wrist and Sid dropped to the ground. With one claw-like hand, the Professor rushed forward and tugged at the fastener of Maggie's rucksack until it came undone.

"You're hurting my wrist," yelled Colin, trying to twist out of the Professor's grasp.

A shower of pebbles fell down the cliff.

"Keep still, Colin!" shouted Maggie.

Sid edged forward on the ground.

"Stay where you are boy!" shouted Professor Falconer at Sid. He reached into Maggie's rucksack with his free hand. A look of triumph and greed spread over his face.

"Why, what have we here?" he said lifting out the golden yellow dragon's egg.

156

"No!" shouted Sid, and launched himself at Professor Falconer's spindly legs. Professor Falconer staggered sideways and dropped Colin to the ground. As Sid charged at him again the Professor stepped quickly to one side and Sid almost slid over the edge of the cliff but he just managed to stretch out his hand and grab Colin's jacket. Using all his strength, Colin managed to pull Sid to safety. Then the twins stared into each other's eyes for a few seconds. A ruby red egg had fallen out of Sid's jacket pocket.

Maggie put her hand up to her throat and touched the gold chain she had been given by Madam Verity the Fortune Teller. She heard *Keesoo's* beautiful voice in her head: *"Trust the Golden Eagle."* Holding her own tiny golden eagle charm, Maggie called out as loudly as she could, "Help us, *Keesoo!* Please come now and help us!"

Professor Falconer took a long, greedy look at the ruby red egg shimmering on the ground. "Another one!" he whispered. "Where are you little horrors getting them from? What are they made of?" He picked up the little red egg. Now he had a dragon's egg in the palm of each hand.

Mike and Maggie exchanged a look. "Go for it, Maggie!" shouted Mike, and they both launched themselves at the Professor. She felt a burst of anger that took her by surprise. *How dare he threaten us,* she thought, and impulsively ran at him again, this time shoving him hard in the chest. "No-one hurts my family!" she screamed.

Professor Falconer staggered and threw out his arms to catch at a tree. The two eggs fell from his grasp and rolled onto the ground. He thrust forward and picked up the red one, but Emma managed to kick the golden yellow one away. Maggie dived on it and put it safely in her pocket. Professor Falconer staggered towards her, but then his foot caught on a tree root and he yelped with pain. With a look of horror he swayed backwards, losing his balance. Then there was a loud crack! Professor Falconer's mouth opened in a silent scream as he tipped over onto the narrow path, landing heavily on his skinny bottom. The red egg flew from his hand and soared through the air. They all stared as it plunged over the edge of the cliff path, falling down and down and down, to land with a splash in the deep pool far below.

"No..oo..oooo!" shouted Sid.

"No..oo..oooo!" shouted Professor Falconer, twisting round to peer over the edge of the cliff path, holding onto a scrubby tuft of grass as he did so. But the grass gave way and, with an awful scream, Professor Falconer plunged head first over the edge of the cliff.

Mike lay down carefully and peered over the crumbling edge of the path. "Stay back you kids!" he ordered.

"Is he dead?" asked Emma.

"No…" said Mike, "…he's lying on the rocks and he's breathing. It looks like one of his legs may be broken. Now, I want you all to do *exactly* as I say."

The rest of the children nodded.

"Emma, twins, you go back to Nanny and Rick and get help," said Mike. "This is the middle of nowhere and we've got to get him to hospital - and also get the police. Maggie, you stand at the top of the cliff and watch him. I'm going to trek over to that forest ranger lodge on the other side of the falls and tell them."

"What about my red egg?" said Sid.

"We'll have to worry about that later," said Maggie. "Now off you both go with Emma. You've all been incredibly brave and I'm ever so proud of you."

"But if we speak to any grown-ups everyone's going to find out about the dragons' eggs," said Sid.

"Yeah," said Colin. "What are we going to do?"

"Try not to mention the eggs to anyone for now," said Maggie. "We've got to trust that things will work out. We've got no choice."

*****

"What's happened? Are any of you hurt?!" Nanny Gardner shouted in alarm when she saw Emma and the twins running towards her.

"Why aren't the others with you?" demanded Rick.

Emma explained to them about Professor Falconer falling off the cliff.

Nanny looked very shocked indeed. "That awful man *again*!?"

"I'll go and fetch Maggie and Mike safely back, Georgina," said Rick to Nanny and he jogged off down the path.

"Whatever's been going on?" said Nanny. "I'll never forgive myself if anything bad has happened. I shouldn't have left you to your own devices. You are going to sit down with me in the van and tell me *everything!*"

*****

Maggie stood on the cliff path looking down at Professor Falconer. His left leg certainly was twisted at a very funny angle. Then she saw a sudden movement and a flash of colour as three Red Kites soared in the sky, circling over Professor Falconer. Each bird dropped something out of its beak. As suddenly as they had appeared, they swerved and flew away along the

159

valley. Maggie craned her neck to try and discover what the birds had dropped. Eggs! Three of them! All smashed to smithereens and covering Professor Falconer's biker's jacket in broken shell and runny yolk!

"Are you okay, Maggie?" called a voice. Rick suddenly appeared with Autumn. "Where is the old man…?" Rick asked, peering over the edge. "Yep, that sure looks nasty. He's been knocked out cold by the look of it. And what's he got splattered all over his coat?"

"Red Kites' eggs," said Maggie. "Look, here comes Mike!"

"Forest rangers have called ambulance and police!" puffed Mike, as he ran towards them.

"Well done, mate. You both get back to the van right now," said Rick. "I'll keep an eye on this character until help arrives."

As Maggie and Mike walked away Mike said, "The forest ranger mentioned something that gave me a good idea. They get lots of people trying to steal rare birds eggs round here. We can tell the grown-ups that was what Professor Falconer was up to when he fell!"

"Brilliant idea! We can only hope the other kids haven't said anything about *our* eggs!" said Maggie
.

*****

"So this terrible man was trying to steal rare birds' egg. Is that right?" asked Nanny Gardner.

"Blooming egg collectors!" said Rick. "Thieves! They'll do anything to add to their collection, or sell them abroad for vast sums of money."

The other children sat silent and wide-eyed. They realised that Maggie and Mike had made up a brilliant story to explain the strange events. Luckily, they had managed to avoid Nanny's probing questions till now.

"So it was red kite eggs he was after all along!" said Nanny, "And the proof is splattered all over him. Those poor birds are only just managing to get re-established up here in Wales. Life for them would be so much easier without people like him interfering."

"It would be easier for all of us…" muttered Mike.

"Well!" said Nanny, "I think it's very honourable of you all to try to stop him stealing birds' eggs but you put yourselves in terrible danger, and you shouldn't have been anywhere *near* that river. It was very brave but, in future, if you see anything like that again, you go and get an adult to deal with it. I shudder to think what could have happened to you."

*****

"A shower of rain!" cried the old white dragon. "And I can feel it soaking into my back! Oh, rain! Oh, oh, wonderful rain!" He stretched his limbs, turned over to wriggle on his back and waved his legs in the air, thrashing his tail as he did so. Opening his eyes, he looked sadly around him. "Oh, I was only dreaming," he said. "It was all just another dream." He sighed and closed his eyes. "Water," he said, tasting the word. "Water must be an amazing thing."

*****

Dave and Holly had rushed back from school. Up in Holly's room, all the children were discussing what had happened.

Holly said, "We have to do something! We haven't got seven eggs any more!"

161

"Is the Stone Egg still going to rise?" asked Emma.

"Will the dragons be cross with us?" asked Colin.

"It wasn't my fault he took it," said Sid.

"It wasn't *anybody's* fault," said Maggie.

"What do we say to the police if they ask us about the Professor?" said Mike.

"We just tell them what Nanny and Rick believe - that he was stealing birds' eggs."

"I don't like telling fibs," said Emma. "I always go red."

"Okay," said Maggie, "well in that case would you rather we say that birds turn into fairies, and bats turn into little golden men, and the Earth lays a Stone Egg every ten thousand years which is going to turn into a new planet when the dragons' eggs hatch?"

They all laughed loudly.

"You're right!" Emma agreed. "They wouldn't believe us, would they?"

"We'll have to ask the Egg Keepers or the Dragon Speakers what to do next," suggested Mike.

"Are you okay, Sid?" said Holly. "You're very quiet."

"I've lost my egg," said Sid gloomily. "You've still all got yours."

"You can share mine," said Colin. "We're twins, after all."

Well, that's certainly a first! The twins actually sharing something! thought Maggie.

"Thanks, Colin," Sid said, and managed a smile.

"Supper's ready, guys!" called Auntie Janie from downstairs. "After all the excitement we're going to spend a nice peaceful evening watching television!"

They all trooped downstairs and Uncle Charles switched the TV on. The newsreader was saying that a Golden Eagle had been spotted in Wales.

162

"Wow, we've got a Golden Eagle in the mountains!" said Uncle Charles "Fancy that!"

"Look at that! It's *our* mountain!" said Maggie. "There are hundreds of people up there!"

"And a bit of news just coming in," the newsreader went on. "A man has been arrested today in connection with the theft of a number of rare Red Kites' eggs. He is believed to be helping police with their enquiries."

"Hope they throw the book at him," said Rick. "Nasty character. He wants locking up. Shall we see if there's a film on?"

"Oh, by the way everyone," said Nanny. "I almost forgot with all the excitement. I've invited an old friend over tomorrow for a spot of lunch. I hope you don't mind, Janie?"

*****

That night, Maggie dreamed that she was swimming in a vast icy cold lake high up in the mountains. Other creatures were swimming beneath the surface of the water and Maggie knew she needed to speak to them and so she dived down to make contact, but every time she caught up with them the other creatures dived even deeper, sinking further and further into the murky depths. *They're like mermaids,* she thought.

Suddenly she found that she could breathe underwater and so she followed the sea creatures through a cave entrance into a huge chamber which shone with a green light that was coming from the mouth of a giant inky black lizard that lay curled up in the centre. The lizard's loud snores shook the floor of the underwater cave, sending ripples through the water. Maggie turned to speak to the sea creatures but they swam away from her into the lizard's mouth and disappeared. Maggie swam

163

after them but stopped suddenly. She didn't want to go inside the lizard's mouth after them, so she leaned against the huge head and looked inside the gaping jaws. "I must try to be brave and follow them," she thought but, just as she was about to swim inside, she glanced at the lizard's face. He had woken up and she found herself gazing into a huge watery red eye. Somehow she knew this creature. She knew it was trapped in the dark, that it was very, *very* angry, and terribly, *terribly* jealous of something.

Maggie woke up with a start. With relief, she could hear the birds singing and knew it was the morning of another day and that there was still enough time left to organise The Rising.

*****

Faraway under the waves, the creature in the deep raised its head. It made a low rumbling noise in its throat that sent shock waves through the water and unsettled the sea for miles around.

*****

Chapter 7

Tunnels and Terrors

Tuesday.

Nanny Gardner had lots of plans to keep the other children busy in the house after Dave and Holly had reluctantly set off for school.

"Janie and Charles have both gone into work. So you can do the dusting," she said to Maggie, "and you two," she said to Sid and Colin, "can help Rick take all the rugs into the garden, hang them over the line and beat them to get the dust out. Cheer up, the pair of you. You're safe now. And Mike..." she went on. "Clear the fire place out, fetch some more logs and kindling and get the stove going please. When you've done that, you can help the twins put the rugs back neatly and straighten the furniture. Emma, you can help me out in the kitchen. I'm doing a roast."

"Let's get it all done as quickly as we can," whispered Maggie to Mike. "She may let us go out for an hour if she's really pleased with us and we can go and fish the red egg out of the river!"

They worked until the whole place shone.

"Shall we take Autumn for a quick walk?" said Maggie to Nanny. "We won't be long."

But there was a knock at the door. Nanny opened it and shrieked with delight. She ushered a lady into the kitchen. The children stared wide-eyed. It was Madam Verity the fortune teller!

"Don't stand there with your mouths open," said Nanny. "Come and greet Verity!"

Verity was smiling. "Hello, children," she said, coming towards them. "We meet again!"

The old white dragon sat once more at his desk to write. "Who is sending me these thoughts," he said to himself. "I can see it all. I can see the scene before me. I can hear the birds singing. My life is changing so much now. What does my future hold? He smiled. It was a sensation he had never experienced before. He put his hand up to his wrinkled cheek, and smiled again. It felt good.

And he wrote…

The Battle of Hastings

A green-eyed girl who lived in Normandy
Could see the future in her head, unsought.
She said, "A mighty battle will be fought
This coming year, Ten sixty six A.D."
She also said, "Our world will bear a child,
An egg of stone, with dragons for a cloak."
The ones who heard her thought it was a joke.
On battlefields of Hastings, no one smiled.
They wove a picture of the great event.
She stitched the egg into a tapestry.
No-one who saw it knew what she had meant,
But she trusted, one day, someone else would see.
She saw more things - things no one would believe.
She told the birds on one bright New Year's Eve.

*****

"I didn't realise you'd all met at the music festival," said Nanny Gardner in surprise, "These are my grandchildren and my almost-grandchildren. Their Mums are twins, you see."

"How lovely!" said Verity. "They're a very special family, Georgina."

"Who's Georgina?" asked Colin.

"That's Nanny Gardner, idiot," said Sid.

Seeing Verity and Nanny together the children noticed how alike they were in their bright, colourful clothes, but whereas Nanny Gardner was average size, Verity was really tiny. Dressed in turquoise velvet from head to toe, she looked, Maggie thought, like a little tropical bird. She could easily see why Madam Verity and Nanny had become lifelong friends.

"Have you seen today's paper, by the way?" Verity said, "You're all in it, children!"She held out the newspaper with a picture of the children and the headline:

Kids nab Egg-Napper. The Yolk's on Him!

"We're in the paper!" said Mike. "Fantastic!"

"Why don't you show Verity round the garden," said Nanny, "while Rick and I set the table for lunch. Take Autumn with you."

And so the children strolled round the garden with Madam Verity the Fortune Teller.

"Do we mention all those gifts she gave us?" whispered Mike to Maggie under his breath.

"Let's wait and see what she says," replied Maggie.

Verity stopped walking and looked straight at them.

"I have seen many strange pictures in my crystal ball lately," she said, "I think it is time you trust me and tell me all about the Stone Egg."

"You know about the Stone Egg?" exclaimed Maggie, surprised. "What else do you know? We thought it was a big secret!"

"I am a crystal-gazer," said Verity. "Ever since Georgina and I were children we both knew there were strange mysteries in the world. She finds love and meaning in music, birds and animals but I see the miraculous and unfamiliar world that lies deep within the crystal ball. I've known the Egg Keepers for some years now and they have learned to trust me. I also know about the dragons' eggs."

"We thought we were the only people in the world who knew," said Emma.

"I've been so worried, Madam Verity," Maggie said, "because we were supposed to be looking after the dragons' eggs and now we've lost the red one and I don't know what to do."

"And Nanny says we can't go out," said Mike, kicking a tree.

"And we have to go home tomorrow," said Emma. "We nearly went home on Sunday."

"Tell me everything as quickly as you can," said Verity.

*****

"I would dearly love to see the Earth," the old white dragon said. "It must be a good feeling to be a dragon covered in plants, to feel the sun's gentle warmth on one's back and a breeze on one's face. There's no warmth in space, no gentleness, only scorching heat and bitter cold!"

Giving the stars a contemptuous look he turned his chair round so that his back was towards the window. "I don't have to look at you," he shouted at the stars. "I don't!"

*****

After lunch, Verity suggested that Nanny Gardner put her feet up and that she would take the children out for a walk. The children crossed their fingers and toes. After all, the Professor was in custody for egg-stealing. What could possibly go wrong? Nanny agreed that it was a great idea as she was pretty worn out and still had a lot of rehearsing to do with Rick. They had a farewell gig in the local pub that evening.

"We will need the ring I gave to Dave," said Verity, and Holly dashed upstairs to fetch it from Dave's bedside table.

"So the red egg fell into the waterfall pool?" said Verity as they all climbed up the mountain path, "You must have been frantic with worry."

"We're worried we've messed everything up," said Maggie.

"Let's see what we can do," said Verity kindly.

Up on the mountain ridge there were people absolutely everywhere with binoculars and telescopes.

"Bird watchers," said Verity. "There's been a suspected sighting of a Golden Eagle."

"We know," said Holly, "Do you think we'll see it?"

"He's called *Keesoo*, and he's an extra-special Egg Keeper," said Maggie. "They don't realise it's not an actual eagle!"

"Have you got your gold necklace on, Maggie?" asked Verity.

"Yes," said Maggie. "Why?"

"I think you need to call your friend *Keesoo*," replied Verity, "So we had better get away from this crowd."

They walked a long way down through the woods away from the birdwatchers.

"Try calling him now, Maggie," said Verity when they were standing in a clearing. "I think the trees will protect us for a short while."

Maggie held the little Golden Eagle charm on her necklace and called, "*Keesoo*. Can you hear me…?"

"It hasn't worked," said Mike.

"Give him a chance to get here," said Verity. "He may be many miles away."

Sure enough, after a few minutes the great golden bird landed on the ground at their feet with a whoosh of feathers.

"Hah!" said *Keesoo*. "How's it going, Gatherers? Greetings Crystal Gazer!"

Verity bowed her head and smiled.

"We don't know what to do about the red egg," said Maggie.

"Yes, I agree, it is a problem," said *Keesoo*. "I wasn't quick enough to stop it sinking deep into the pool. The Dippers and Kingfishers have searched there for two days with no luck."

"What's a Dipper?" asked Emma.

"A small diving bird," replied Verity.

"There must be *something* we can do!" said Mike.

"I think," said *Keesoo,* "we need to talk to the Lady of the Lake."

"She doesn't exist!" said Mike a little scornfully. "It's just an old story Nanny told us."

"Oh yes she does!" said *Keesoo*. "Her name is Azura. She's a bit snooty but she'll probably help out."

"Wow! Let's go *now!*" said the twins, jumping up and down.

171

"Alright," said Verity. "I'll tell Georgina I'm driving you all to see the Golden Eagle. It's what we call in my trade a bit of a fib."

"I never tell fibs!" said Colin.

"Me neither!" said Sid.

"I'll race you," said *Keesoo* as he took off.

"Why did you give those little gifts to us?" asked Emma.

"Are they magic?" asked Sid.

"Questions, questions, questions," laughed Verity, "A pair of strange cave creatures in my crystal ball told me to give them to you. The rings and the necklace have been in my family for generations, handed down to me. As for what they can do, I don't know. I am just the messenger."

*****

Verity parked her car beside a laurel bush on the lane leading to the lake. She wasn't as good a driver as Rick or Nanny Gardner and they had spent most of the journey holding on to one another for dear life.

"It's a bit of a walk," declared Verity, as they climbed the mountain path and struggled over the crest. They stumbled across a vast yellowy green pasture down to the shores of the deep blue lake where, much to the children's relief, they found *Keesoo* perched on a rock.

"What kept you?" he said, and grinned at them.

"What now, *Keesoo*?" panted Maggie as they all collapsed on the ground.

"You must collect herbs," said *Keesoo*, "comfrey, agrimony, yarrow, thyme, oregano, meadowsweet, violets, vervain, anything aromatic."

"What's arrowmatick?" asked Colin.

"What's any of it?" asked Sid.

172

"It means the special way herbs smell," said Mike.

"But we don't know what on earth they all look like," said Maggie, "I only know what parsley is. Mum uses it in cooking."

"I will recognise them," said Verity.

"And kindling for a fire," said *Keesoo*, "dry seed heads, twigs, scraps of sheep's wool, small pieces of wood."

They all scattered in different directions.

"How are we doing, *Keesoo?*" asked Emma after a while, dashing up and dumping an armful of twigs in front of him.

"That should do it," *Keesoo* said.

"Has anyone got any matches?" said Maggie.

"I think," said *Keesoo*, "that Mike can help us with this. We will need Dave's amber ring that you carry in your pocket. I want you to point the ring towards the kindling and imagine it burning. Focus your mind on the stone," said *Keesoo*.

Mike stood awkwardly pointing the copper ring with the amber stone at the pile of wood, frowning with concentration, imagining bright flames leaping up from the damp kindling.

After a few seconds, *Keesoo* said, "That's done it!"

They all blinked. Sparks shooting from Mike's finger were landing on the pile of kindling. Wisps of smoke were rising from it as a small flame crackled into life. Soon the fire was blazing.

"Wow!" said Mike. "Did I really do that?"

"Now throw on the herbs," said *Keesoo*.

As they threw the leaves onto the fire, a wonderful aroma filled the air.

"Now we must call the Lady Azura," said *Keesoo*. "Mike, we need you again."

"Here!" said Mike, leaping forward.

"Point the finger with your own silver ring at the lake and call out, 'My Lady'," said *Keesoo*. "Always address her as 'My Lady.' She likes to be treated as if she's royalty."

Mike took a step forward and, feeling like a hero in a movie, he swept a low bow, flung his head back and raised his arm to point.

"My Lady," he called. "We need to speak to you!"

A white mist from the blue stone in the ring drifted like a long boney finger towards the edge of the lake. The mist looked like a silvery rippling path that sat upon the surface of the lake. As they watched, out of the water and along the path walked a majestic figure. She was wearing sky blue robes that floated like waves as she moved across the water.

"Wow!" said Mike.

The woman stepped onto the shore and walked to where Verity and the children stood. She was very graceful, with hair as fine and fair as the morning mist, and she sparkled in the sunlight like a melting icicle.

"Who calls to Azura with perfumed smoke?" the woman asked.

"We do, My Lady," said Maggie in a shaky voice.

"We need your help, My Lady," said *Keesoo,* bowing very low. "We have lost a red egg belonging to the dragons."

"And why should I help the dragons?" asked Azura, sticking her nose in the air.

"May I respectfully remind you, My Lady," said *Keesoo*, "that I am *Keesoo*, Most High King of the Egg Keepers, Ultimate Ruler of the skies, Chief Guardian of the Day, and, more importantly, an old friend of your father's. I ask this in return for the favour I once did him."

"What is it that you want from me?" said Azura.

"We need to know," said *Keesoo*, "if any of your people have seen the red egg."

"Yes, we have seen the red egg," replied Azura. "Some of my people played with it when it first arrived in our world and told me it was a pretty toy. They chased it down the river, among the rocks, over many waterfalls until they became bored with it and lost it as it drifted out to sea. I am so sorry but that is all I can tell you. I can help you no more."

"Thank you for your time, My Lady," *Keesoo* said. "Please convey my good wishes to your father. I am grateful."

Azura bowed her head and turning her back on them, walked down to the shores of the lake and then deeper and deeper into the water until the ripples closed over her head.

*****

The creature at the bottom of the ocean turned slowly round, choosing its position with care. With great difficulty it lowered itself until it was lying once more on the seabed. It rested its long dark blue head on the sand and its eyes, half closed, took on a crafty look, like a snake watching its prey. It opened its mouth, a vast cave surrounded by sharp curved red teeth. Its black tongue spread out so that it looked less like a tongue and more like a layer of black mud on the floor of the cave. The creature waited. It was good at waiting.

*****

"Oh!" said Emma. "Wasn't she beautiful?"

"Full of airs and graces," muttered *Keesoo*. "They all fancy themselves, these Water People. They need to live in the real world for a while, they do! They've either lost the red egg or they've actually hidden it for later. A pretty toy to play with indeed! I did not believe a word she said!"

"We've tried, children," said Verity. "I am still sure everything will work out for the best. I saw seven dragons in a dream last night. I feel certain that something useful will happen soon."

"Have the dragons laid all their other eggs yet, *Keesoo?*" asked Emma.

"Yes, but they will remain underground," said *Keesoo*. "They are no substitute for The Seven. I must continue the search for the red egg. Goodbye." He leapt into the air.

"Throw some water on that fire, will you children?" said Verity. "I'd better get you all safely back home!"

*****

"I would have had great forests on my back," said the old white dragon, stretching himself out in the dust. "Or maybe I'd have been a craggy, snow covered mountain, or a grassy hill carpeted with wild flowers. People would have said, 'Here's a fine mountain. Let's climb it. Let's build a castle on its back.'" He smiled to himself at the thought. "Or I might have been a mountain under the sea," he went on, "with just my back sticking out above the waves to form an island. I could have watched the underwater creatures swimming by and felt the sun on my back. Yes, I'd have enjoyed that."

He arranged his legs and tail to form majestic slopes.
Then he stretched out his long nose, flaring his nostrils
to form two dark caves. He felt quite happy as he lay
there in the dust imagining these things - happier, in
fact, than he'd felt for thousands of years.

*****

"Autumn, stay!" ordered Maggie as soon as the children had finished stacking their board games on the floor of the tree house. But they hadn't really been playing the board games – once Dave and Holly had got home from school they had actually organised an important planning meeting. Autumn had lain down by the foot of the ladder and was resting her head on her paws.

"Right," said Maggie. "I've told Autumn to stay here. Nanny will see her and think we're all still up in the tree house. But we have to be as quick as we can as time is getting on! Let's go!"

Hurrying up the hillside and scrambling into the stone circle, all seven children settled themselves against their special guardian stones.

"What's supposed to happen now?" asked Holly.

"I'm hoping we'll get some sort of clue what to do next," said Maggie.

"Last time we had a shared dream so let's see if we can do that again."

"But I'm not sleepy," said Emma.

"Let's close our eyes anyway," replied Maggie.

"Do you think the gifts Verity gave us can do any other sort of magic?" said Mike. "That was so cool the way your ring started the fire, Dave!"

"Yeah...I bet..." said Dave, feeling rather left out, "Wish I'd been there!"

177

"Colin and me have got our key rings with us!" said Sid.

"It would be good if we could make two dragons come out of one egg just like our key rings," said Colin.

"Maybe if you hold them together," said Maggie, "it might help. Now all stop talking and close your eyes."

Maggie soon felt herself falling asleep. Immediately, or so it seemed, she was hovering above the circle. She could see the others below her, also fast asleep. Floating beside her, holding her hand, was the dream girl she had seen in the meadow.

"Don't be afraid," said the dream-girl. "We are going to the centre of the sun. Close your eyes."

Maggie felt the air around her getting warmer and through her closed eyelids could see a bright yellow glow.

"Now," said the dream girl, "open your eyes."

Maggie and the other children were standing in a yellow room at the centre of which stood a huge golden dragon, his body swirling as if made of fire, the scales on his back flickering like flames around coals, his eyes like molten gold.

"Hello, my child," he said in a voice that sounded like a crackling bonfire. He reached out a golden claw and touched Maggie's forehead. His claw felt ice-cold.

"It is an honour to meet you. You are going to save the world, Maid Maggie, but first you must face the things you fear most. For this purpose have the dragons and the Earth chosen you. We know you will succeed."

"What do I have to do?" asked Maggie, shivering with worry.

"You must find those that speak for the dragons and for the Earth but are ignored by both," said the golden dragon.

"I don't understand you!" exclaimed Maggie.

"Then you must ask those who will understand," said the golden dragon. "The two who once were one hold the one that must become two. But it is vital that you go alone. The other Guardians cannot assist you. Do you hear me, child?"

Maggie nodded, but she was no clearer than before.

"One more thing before you go," whispered the golden dragon. "When the White Moon Dragon flies and all is well once more, your task is finished. But for now, that is something you must forget. You will remember it again when the time comes. Goodbye."

Maggie and the dream girl bowed to the golden dragon and at once found themselves floating in soft violet light, drifting back past planets inhabited by strange creatures. Now and then, as she floated by, she caught a glimpse of a fair-haired girl exactly like herself looking back at her. Did the little Victorian girl look like this? Were all the little chosen girls exactly the same? How many worlds and bright suns were there in one universe? Hundreds? Thousands? More than that?

"How can I still breathe here in outer space?" thought Maggie. *"How is that possible?"*

They flew past solar systems and lonely stars in the indigo darkness. Then they arrived suddenly at planet Earth where they fell from clear blue sky through green hazy foliage into the golden glow of sunshine, sinking down, down, down into the rich orangey brown soil, all the way through the earth to its centre, where fire glowed red. And where a voice said...

We speak for the dragons.
We speak for the earth.
The spring will cause one
To be two at the birth.

179

It was a voice Maggie had heard before. It was the same strange voice that had whispered to her deep inside the rainbow mountain!

Maggie felt terror strike her heart like a blow from a fist. Then she was travelling upwards among the curling red flames and the rich rust-red earth, and out into the sunlight. Her heart was beating very fast, pounding in her chest, and there was a strange metallic taste in her mouth. She screwed her eye lids tightly shut.

When she opened them again, she was sitting safely in the stone circle, the other children still around her. But their faces were concerned. Emma was nearly crying, the twins were hopping about frantically and Mike was holding her hand.

"I've had another dream," murmured Maggie.

"Nightmare, more like!" said Dave. "What happened to you? I woke up feeling great but then you started thrashing about and screaming your head off!"

"My dream was really nice," said Emma, gulping back tears. "I floated up through a rainbow to a golden bubble but I was still worried about you, Maggie. You seemed to go off on your own without us!"

"I floated like that too," said Sid. "Maggie, I saw you inside a big golden ball with a big yellow dragon!"

"Yeah, I saw that too," shouted Colin. "You looked a bit worried!"

"That's exactly what I saw," agreed Mike.

"Then I whooshed down again like a spaceship and landed back in the circle," said Holly.

"Didn't you go inside the Earth then?" asked Maggie.

They all shook their heads.

"You must have been chosen for something else, Maggie," said Dave quietly.

"The golden dragon said I have to face my worst fears," said Maggie. "To save the world I have to speak

180

to those that speak for the dragons and the Earth, but are ignored by both."

"What on earth does *that* mean?" said Mike.

"I have no idea," said Maggie. "He said I must ask those who will understand."

"That will be the Egg Keepers," said Emma.

"Or the Dragon Speakers," agreed Holly. "They're bound to know!"

"I suppose so," said Maggie. "He also said that the two who once were one hold the one that must be two.' And he said I must go on my own," she shuddered as she remembered.

"You said if you had another dream, you might find what you need to do," said Dave. "I think it's very clear that you've been told *exactly* what to do."

"Only if I can work out what it means!" said Maggie. She was beginning to feel as if the weight of the whole world was resting on her shoulders. The others meant well, but they couldn't help her face her fears alone could they?

"We'd better get back home," said Mike. "Nanny Gardner might be checking up on us by now. Let's sit in the tree house and decide what to do next."

But, suddenly, there was a whoosh of wings over their heads. Sitting on the top of Maggie's guardian stone was *Keesoo*. Maggie felt tearful with relief and told him all about the dream. *Keesoo* listened carefully, frowned and rubbed his chin.

"I can see no way that we Egg-Keepers can help you with this," said *Keesoo*.

"But the golden dragon at the centre of the sun said someone would know!" exclaimed Maggie. "I thought he must have meant you!"

"I am so sorry, Maid Maggie." His voice was grave, "You have to go alone."

"But go *where*?" asked Maggie. It was horrible to be the one with all the responsibility.

Keesoo looked very thoughtful, "We'll speak with *Barglor*," he said "Then, together with the Dragon Speakers, it is possible we can work out what to do." He turned to the other children.

"You must go home, six guardians," he said. "Maggie is required to do this mission on her own this very night. We will do our very best to protect her."

"Surely *one* of us could go with her!" said Mike, "just to keep watch over her?"

"No," said *Keesoo* firmly. "You six must go home. There isn't much time. You had better bring the egg, Maid Maggie."

"What egg?!" asked Maggie, secretly hoping something might happen to stop her going anywhere.

"The green one, of course!" said *Keesoo*. "The one that must be two."

"Because we're the two who once were one!" yelled Sid, really pleased that he had worked this out!

"Because we're identical twins!" shouted Colin. "We came from the same egg too!"

"Here," said Colin, taking the green egg from his pocket and giving it to Maggie.

"Look after it, Maggie," said Sid.

"We'll see you later, Maggie," said Mike softly, "I'm really sorry I can't go for you."

"So am I," said Maggie, and then managed a smile. "Off you all go then. I'll be home as soon as I can. If Nanny Gardner asks where I am, tell her…tell her…" but she was racking her brains. What could they *possibly* tell her?

"Time seems to stand still on these occasions," said Dave thoughtfully. "Maybe you won't be gone for very

182

long at all. Maybe you'll be back with us in minutes or even seconds."

"If Nanny asks we'll think of something," said Holly kindly.

The six children set off down the mountain path towards home. Each time they turned back to look, Maggie and *Keesoo* were deep in conversation. And, as they went round the last corner, Mike took one last worried look back. Maggie and *Keesoo* were gone.

*****

"I would have had caves," said the white dragon out loud. "I would have had great underground caverns with magnificent stalactites and stalagmites and deep, dark lakes. I might have had seams of bright metals running through my walls or maybe they would be lined with crystals that sparkled when they caught the light. I might have had freshwater springs making waterfalls down my sides, and rivers bubbling over the rocks all the way down to the tip of my tail."

He flicked his long tail to and fro, creating clouds of white dust around him.

"If I hadn't been stuck here, that's what I'd have done," said the old white dragon.

*****

Keesoo walked over to the rock. He was speaking in a series of warbles and clicks. The door in the rock slid open and *Barglor* appeared looking ruffled, his hand over his eyes to shield them from the sunshine. *Keesoo* and *Barglor* spoke in whispers for a few minutes and then *Barglor* flew back into the tunnel.

"You must go now," said *Keesoo* to Maggie. "*Barglor* has agreed to take you to speak with the dragons. Be very brave, Maid Maggie. Good luck."

He bowed to Maggie, flung his cloak around his shoulders and flew off.

Maggie took a deep breath, stepped through the doorway and braced herself to face the tunnel and whatever else was ahead of her.

If I hear that weird whispering voice now, I'm running for my life, she thought. *Someone else can save the world!*

Barglor flew a little ahead of her and they reached the crystal cave. Then he flew across to the Speaking Stone, talking to it in a low mutter as he landed. He beckoned to her to come over to join him. Maggie felt very small indeed as she walked alone across the cave. Her legs were shaking as she rested her hands on the Speaking Stone. Although she was expecting it, the trembling of the stone and the rasping dragon's voice still made her jump out of her skin.

"Our faith in you is well placed," wheezed the voice. "Now we will tell you a secret. There are only two creatures in the universe that have the ability to speak for we dragons as well as for the Earth. They are nothing to us but they may have the answer you seek. They may wish to earn our gratitude."

"Who are they?" asked Maggie, not sure she actually wanted to know.

"They call themselves the Lava-Eaters," rasped the dragon's voice, shaking the stone.

"But who *are* they?" asked Maggie anxiously, "and where will I find them?"

"We do not speak to them," spat the dragon. "You must ask them what you want to know. *Barglor* will show you the way."

184

The vibrations in the rock ceased as the dragon left. Maggie turned to *Barglor*.

"I've really got to do this, haven't I?" she asked.

"Yes, if we are to save the world," said *Barglor*.

"Then you'd better lead the way," said Maggie bravely, but she was thinking, *I don't think I've ever been more scared in my entire life!*

Her legs still shaking, her teeth chattering and her mouth so dry that she had to keep swallowing, she followed *Barglor* to the far side of the crystal cave. He spoke a few gurgling syllables and a tunnel entrance opened in the wall.

"Good luck, Maid Maggie," announced *Barglor*.

"Is that it?" spluttered Maggie. "You're not coming with me any further than this? What do I do now? I don't want to walk alone down a dark tunnel without knowing anything about where I'm going! Who am I meeting!? And how I'm supposed to get out again!?"

"This is the way it must be," said *Barglor* firmly.

Maggie felt a rush of anger.

"Suppose I *don't* do it?" she raged. "Suppose I change my mind, walk away. Go home! Forget I ever met any of you?!"

"We cannot make you do this," said *Barglor*. "The world will end. No one will ever know you didn't go."

"You're making it out to be all my fault now!" shouted Maggie, "Trying to make me feel guilty!"

"No, child…" said *Barglor* softly, "I am doing none of those things." He perched on a ledge and put his head in his hands. He looked so very sad that Maggie's heart ached for him.

"Well, alright, I'll try. But I expect you to wait here for me," Maggie said. "Don't you *dare* go anywhere, understand?" *Barglor* raised his head, smiled gratefully at her, and nodded.

Taking a deep breath, she stepped into the tunnel. It smelled of stale air, like rotting leaves or wet dogs mingled with something sickly like treacle pudding. The walls, when she touched them, were slimy, and her fingers sometimes found something small that wriggled. Her eyes struggled to see, making the darkness sparkle with a million tiny fireworks. She felt her way one step at a time, her hands outstretched.

"Hello?" she called, her voice very shaky. "Is there anybody there?"

This is certainly what I fear most, she thought. *I'm supposed to feel so honoured to be chosen to do this - NOT!!"*

Then she heard a slithering, scraping noise.

"Who's there?" she whispered, her heart beating loudly in her chest.

She shouted out as a hand touched her arm. Then she stood frozen in her tracks, far too frightened to move. Her ears were pounding and she fought back the urge to be sick.

"Who are you…I…I can't see you!" she croaked.

Her knees turned to jelly as she heard a low, deep voice from the tunnel reply, "We'll light the lamps for you..." Then the hand left her arm, there was a scuffling noise and a flame flickered into life in a candle-holder on the wall. In the dim shadowy light Maggie could make out a cave whose walls were covered with colourful paintings of animals and whose floor was uneven with many glistening puddles. Then, very gradually, as her eyes adjusted to the light, she could make out a man and a woman. They were thick-set and shuffling slowly along, lighting lamps around the walls, illuminating the cave a bit at a time. As the light grew brighter and brighter the two figures turned round and started to walk towards her. Maggie couldn't help herself. She screamed.

*****

"I wonder if there is another dragon anywhere like me?" said the old white dragon, looking at the star-filled sky. "Am I the only dragon in the universe that hasn't got a world of its own? There are so many stars. How many worlds must there be circling them? There must be other moons out there. I think I'd feel better if I thought that out there somewhere, there was another dragon like me."

*****

The creature under the sea closed its mouth, swallowing something that had accidentally drifted in. A look of sly satisfaction spread over its crumpled indigo face. The sea around it was empty of life. Nothing went near it and it lay like a pile of dirty laundry on the abandoned ocean floor.

*****

The six children walked down the cliff path in silence. It was unbearable leaving Maggie to face such a challenge on her own but they had no choice. When they reached the tree house they looked around. Autumn had gone.

"She never goes off when Maggie tells her to stay!" exclaimed Mike.

"We've *got* to find her!" said Colin.

"Maggie will be ever so cross if we don't!" said Sid.

"I do hope Maggie's okay…" sobbed Emma, suddenly very sad and frightened.

"We'll have to go and look for Autumn right now!" said Dave.

"Definitely," said Holly. "Remember that she's in The Legend? I think she's gone to find Maggie!"

They turned around and trudged back up the mountain.

Chapter 8

Dogs and Discoveries

The man and woman were now standing in front of Maggie. Their skin was the colour and texture of crocodile hide. Their faces had flattened noses, and their foreheads were low and ridged. They had thin blackened lips like a cleft in a rock. Their hair, if it was hair at all, stuck up in sharp green spikes. Their large eyes were watery and brown. Maggie felt her own scalp tingle with fear.

"You're the first human we've seen since before the Ice Age," one of the creatures wheezed, holding out a claw-like hand.

Maggie backed away, trying to speak, but her words stuck in her throat. She coughed. "Are you the Lava-Eaters?" she finally managed to croak.

"We are the Lava-Eaters," replied one of the creatures. "My name is Deev and this is Adma."

"What *are* Lava-Eaters?" asked Maggie. "I don't understand what you're doing here. I've never ever heard of Lava-Eaters. Did you say the Ice Age?!"

"Yes. We've been here many thousands of years," said Deev, "We were living in these caves when the Ice Age came."

"But what exactly are you doing down here?" said Maggie, so puzzled she was forgetting to be frightened.

"We're humans like you," said Adma, "or at least we were back then."

"What happened to you?" asked Maggie.

"There was a rock slide," said Deev, "We were trapped for days, starving and desperate. Then we found a green egg. We didn't know what it was or why it was there."

"What did you do with it?" asked Maggie, folding her arms over her rucksack which she knew held her own green dragon's egg.

Deev groaned and Adma let out a sobbing cry.

"We ate it!" cried Deev.

"It seems it was a dragon's egg," droned Adma. "Because we ate it, it changed us into something not human. We became something part dragon and part Earth, but we still feel human inside."

"Suddenly we knew special things," said Deev, "We could understand what the dragons were saying and we knew what the Earth was thinking."

"But the dragons wouldn't talk to us," said Adma. "We spoke to them in their language but they ignored us. We told them we were sorry for eating one of their eggs. We begged their forgiveness."

"But they sealed all the doors," said Deev, "They won't ever let us out. Everything the dragons and the Earth know we know *too* but we're shut in here, enduring an everlasting punishment."

"Why are you still alive?" asked Maggie. "How do you survive?"

"We're immortal," said Adma, "That *is* the punishment. We eat lava and drink fire. We have the whole world of caves and tunnels to live in for eternity."

It felt to Maggie as she looked around the dimly lit cave as if the mountain above their heads was pressing down on her.

"I can't imagine a worse nightmare," said Maggie, "than being trapped underground in the dark forever. You poor, poor things."

"Oh, we're used to it now," said Adma, "and we have each other for company."

"There's another creature too," rasped Deev. "We don't know who he is but he is a prisoner just like us."

"We don't see him but we hear him in our heads," said Adma. "We send him poetry."

"Yes, we send him poems with our minds," said Deev. "And he writes it all down in a great book."

"Where is he?" asked Maggie. "Is he a Lava-Eater like you?"

"We don't think so," said Adma. "He feels like a dragon to us but he can't be. The other dragons don't seem to know about him."

"And then there's the other one," said Deev, "the creature whose mind is dark."

"That one doesn't hear us," said Adma, "but we hear him."

"Was it you two who whispered to me in the tunnels?" said Maggie. "You scared me so much."

"We wanted to warn you," said Deev. "We didn't know why you'd come."

"It sounded as if you were laughing at me," said Maggie.

"We were crying for you," said Deev.

"There were too many voices," said Adma. "It scared us. We're not used to human voices. There were so many of you suddenly."

"But we know what is happening now," said Deev. "You have been sent to ask for our help. At last we have a chance to make amends."

"Do you want to give us your green dragon's egg?" asked Adma.

Maggie hesitated. Could this strange pair really be trusted?

"What are you going to do with it?" she asked. "You won't…er…you won't eat it, will you?"

The Lava-Eaters groaned.

"We learned our lesson many, many years ago," Adma said, "We won't be doing that again."

"Come with us," said Deev. "We will show you what we need to do."

"Is it far?" asked Maggie, reluctant to go even deeper underground.

"Only a short boat ride," said Deev.

"Boat ride?" said Maggie anxiously.

"This way," said Adma. "Bring a lighted torch with you if it makes you feel better."

He took one of the flaming torches from the wall and gave it to Maggie who was very grateful for it.

I can't believe how brave I'm being, she thought, *exactly like an intrepid explorer.*

The tunnel was shadowy and winding and led downhill where it opened out into a long, thin cavern. The sides of the cavern were thick with layer upon layer of stalactites, and down the centre was a wide dark river.

Maggie could see a boat tied to a rock by the shore. The boat was intricately woven from tree roots.

I'm going further and further away from Barglor and the mountain path home, she thought and her stomach lurched.

As Adma helped Maggie into the strange boat, she tried not to recoil at the touch of his hard, scaly hand. Then Deev picked up the two twisty wooden paddles and rowed the boat through the black water, skimming in and out of the stalactite-encrusted walls. After what seemed like hours they arrived inside a vast cave that towered above a huge lake. In the centre of the lake was a small island. Deev steered the boat to the island and Adma climbed out and tied it to a stalagmite. He helped Maggie and Deev out and then led Maggie over to a glistening rock-face from which bubbling crystal clear water trickled down into a the dark lake.

"This," said Adma, "is the Spring of the Earth's Tears."

Adma lifted up a grey stone bowl.

"What's that?" asked Maggie.

"Inside this bowl is the tears of many dragons," said Adma, "tears shed while the Dragon Speakers lay dead in the mud."

"The dragons' tears that were saved by the Egg Keepers," said Deev, "in the dark, dark times of what you call The Legend."

"The Egg Keepers are our friends," said Adma. "It is good."

Then Deev scooped up some water from the spring in her cupped hands and added it to Adma's bowl.

"Give me the green egg," said Deev, her watery brown eyes glistening in the light of the torches.

Maggie gave Deev the green egg, thinking, *I have to trust them now or fail.*

Deev took the egg from her, holding it out to Adma. Then, both touching it with their broad fingers, they lowered it down into the water in the bowl. Together they chanted:

We speak for the dragons.
We speak for the earth.
The spring will cause one
To be two at the birth."

"You said that in my dream!" said Maggie, amazed.

"Let one become two," recited Deev and Adma together.

The liquid in the bowl fizzed like sherbet, filling the cave with a perfume that reminded Maggie of Christmas and churches. Then Deev and Adma lifted the egg from the bowl and gave it back to Maggie.

"It is done," said Deev. "Maybe the dragons and the Earth will forgive us now."

"But what will happen next?" asked Maggie.

"This green egg will produce two dragons," said Deev.

"We will return you now to the place where we met," said Adma.

And they helped Maggie back into the boat, paddled back across the lake and then up the river to the tunnel. Maggie's torch had burnt very low and, as she climbed from the boat, it flickered and went out. Maggie felt panic rising in her throat but fought it back.

I've nearly done this, she thought. *Keep going, Maggie, you're doing great.* She made herself smile and then thought of Mum and Dad and that soon she would be going home.

"I'll give you another torch," said Adma's voice and fire flared on a new lamp.

"Thank you," Maggie said as she followed the two Lava-Eaters along the tunnel that led back to the painted cave.

"Your way home is through here," said Deev, pointing to a tunnel.

194

"Thank you for what you've done to help me," said Maggie. "What will you both do next?"

"We will remain here," said Adma. "The dragons and the Earth may forgive us now - which will make our lives less lonely - but we are no longer human. We could not return to life on the surface now. Our home is here."

"That's so sad," said Maggie and reached out her hands to the Lava-Eaters. "I'm very sorry."

Adma and Deev took hold of her hands in their own scaly ones. Maggie felt tears running down her cheeks.

"It has been very good to talk with a human again," said Deev. "Goodbye."

"Good luck," said Adma.

"Goodbye and good luck to you too," said Maggie, "and thank you."

*****

"Dragons don't move around," muttered the old, white dragon. "If there's another dragon out there like me, I'll never meet him. I hate to think of a dragon in the universe as lonely as me, living on some distant moon, looking up at the stars, with maybe a whole world in his imagination that he's never going to see. Poor, poor lonely dragon," He sat on the ground with his head in his claws, rocking to and fro and whimpering softly.

*****

Maggie walked along the tunnel, her hand resting on her bag which held the green egg safe and sound, a faint light from the crystal cave ahead drawing her along. As she reached the tunnel entrance, *Barglor* flew over to land on her shoulder.

195

"Are you safe?!" he asked, excited, "Is it done?!"

"Everything's fine, *Barglor*," said Maggie, "Thank you for waiting for me. I need to go home now because I'm very tired."

Suddenly something launched itself at her, knocking her over.

Autumn!" cried Maggie, as Autumn's tongue washed her face. The dog was delighted to see Maggie.

"She has been waiting at the mouth of the cave for your safe return," said *Barglor*. Maggie sat on the ground cuddling the excited dog and trying not to cry.

"Maggie!" shouted several voices, and she looked up to see the other children rushing along the mountain path towards her. *Barglor* took flight.

"Where have you all been?!" shouted Nanny Gardner's angry voice. She was puffing across the goat field towards them. "I clearly told you not to go anywhere without telling me first! You *promised* me you'd be playing board games in the tree house. What are you all doing out here?"

"We lost Autumn!" replied Colin quickly.

"She ran off!" said Sid nodding.

"We had to go looking for her," said Dave, catching on.

"We've been calling and calling her," said Emma.

"And Maggie found her, so it's alright!" said Holly.

Maggie burst into tears of relief, sitting on the ground, her rucksack slung over her shoulder, her arms around Autumn's neck. Relieved to see her, Mike knelt down beside Maggie and put his arm around her.

"Oh, that silly dog…" exclaimed Nanny. "…she must have been chasing foxes again! You've found her now so do stop crying Maggie. You've all got yourselves hot and bothered over nothing. The dog would have found her way back home soon enough! Come on, kids. Roast chicken for supper!"

*****

"It wasn't as bad as I expected," said Maggie when the children were all gathered in Holly's bedroom after supper. "I was very frightened but there was so much to think about that I sort of forgot to be scared at times - and I felt very sorry for the Lava-Eaters. They were quite sweet really."

"They sound terrifying," said Dave, "Did you say they're half dragon and half human?"

"I think so," said Maggie, "They said they were the only creatures able to understand what the Earth thinks and what the dragons say."

"The only creatures in the universe?" asked Sid, spreading his arms wide.

"Anywhere at all?" asked Colin, spinning round and falling over.

"Yes," said Maggie.

"What was their boat made out of?" asked Emma.

"I don't know, sort of woven roots I think," said Maggie, "But it didn't leak."

"Could you find your way back there?" asked Mike. "I'd love to go exploring around those amazing sounding caves."

"The dragons seal all the doors," said Maggie.

"That's really cruel," said Holly, "They should let the Lava-Eaters out now after everything you've done."

"I don't think they really want to come out," said Maggie, "People would be frightened of them you see, because of the way they look."

"They could pretend they were statues in a park," said Mike, "and just as people were walking past they could run at them, waving their arms and shouting."

Everyone thought that was funny except Maggie. She couldn't stop thinking what a terrible thing it was for Deev and Adma to be shut underground forever.

"Have they done some sort of magic to the green egg?" said Holly.

"Is it going to be twins?" asked Sid.

"Out of one egg, like Sid and me?" asked Colin.

"I think so," said Maggie, quietly. "They said it would all be fine now." But even as she said this, she really wasn't quite so sure that was true.

*****

The old white dragon looked at the dry dusty ground beneath his feet. It was the same dead ground stretching from horizon to horizon, broken only by craters where forgotten rocks had hit the moon's surface. "If only there was some way I could escape from this terrible lonely place," he said.

*****

"My feet hurt," said Emma as they waited for supper to be cooked.

"Let me have a look," said Maggie. "They've been hurting you all week. Maybe your trainers are too small."

"They're quite new," said Emma taking them off.

Maggie picked one of the trainers up and examined it.

"Hey!" she exclaimed in surprise.

Holly picked the other one up and peered at the sole.

"Wow!" she agreed.

198

"What's the big deal?" said Mike, putting down Dave's train magazine.

"Pass me a pencil please, Mike," said Maggie.

"Which one would you like?" asked Mike.

"It doesn't matter," said Maggie. "Just hand me one," She took a pencil from him and used one end of it to dig something out from between the deep treads of Emma's trainer. She found something and held it up to the light.

"What is it?" asked Emma.

"Some sort of crystal, I think," said Maggie. "You must have picked it up on the sole of your shoe in the crystal cave."

"Look, here's another one!" said Holly, peering at the bottom of Emma's other trainer.

"No wonder your feet have been hurting," said Maggie.

"Poor Emma," said Holly.

"More like rich Emma!" said Dave. "That one looks like an emerald to me!"

"An emerald!" said Sid.

"Result!" said Colin.

"You could sell that for a heap of money!" said Mike.

"I think if any of us tried to sell an emerald," said Maggie sternly, "they'd want to know where we got it from."

"Look, here are some more stuck in the other shoe," said Holly.

"That's much better," said Emma, putting her trainers back on. "My feet don't hurt at all now!"

Maggie put the handful of emerald green crystals in the dressing table drawer next to the green egg.

"We don't know they're worth anything really," she said.

Then Maggie gasped. The others all looked at her. She pointed inside the drawer and the others all rushed to look. The green dragons' egg was glowing brightly. It was rocking to and fro and making a loud tapping noise. It was as if it had recognised the green crystals.

"My egg!" shouted Sid when he spotted the green glow.

"Sssshhh!" hissed the girls.

"It's hatching!" exclaimed Colin.

"Cool!" said Sid.

"I've got a dragon's egg hatching into two baby dragons in my bedroom," hissed Holly. "I'm not sure I can cope with this!"

"It's okay," said Dave. "It will be fine, I'm sure."

"Oh good," said Holly glaring at Dave. "I won't worry then!"

They all watched the green egg as the tapping got louder. The egg rocked faster and faster. Then there was a loud crack and a flash of green light. The green egg fell into two halves and out toppled two tiny dragons. One green, one red. Each baby dragon was seven centimeters long and was glistening with golden liquid.

"Two!" whispered Sid.

"Twins!" whispered Colin.

"It worked!" said Maggie, tears coming into her eyes. "It actually *worked*!"

All the children stood transfixed, their hands to their faces, their eyes round, hardly daring to breathe.

The two baby dragons shook themselves and looked about.

"I wasn't expecting them to be so *sweet*!" said Emma.

The twin dragons took their first tottering steps. The red one managed to slip over in some of the golden liquid and fell on his back with his little legs kicking in the air. He struggled to his feet, spread his tiny wings and shook them. The green dragon flapped his wings and took off suddenly, crash-landing onto Holly's pillow. The children gasped. Autumn whined.

"Is it hurt?" whispered Emma.

"No, look. It's sitting up..." whispered Maggie.

The red dragon flew to join the green one. Then they both took off together, flying round and round the room, circling above the children's heads, getting stronger and stronger.

The red one landed on Sid's shoulder. Sid held his breath.

"Awwwhh..." murmured Colin, holding out his hand to the green one.

The green dragon settled on Colin's outstretched hand, swayed a little and then sat down. It bent its tiny head and licked his fingers.

"I've got a red dragon," whispered Sid, with tears in his eyes.

"What's all the commotion about?" said Uncle Charles as he came into the room suddenly. "We're serving supper. Downstairs everyone!"

The children looked at the places where the baby dragons had been sitting. They had completely disappeared from view.

"Sorry, Dad," said Dave. "The girls wanted to know about star constellations and I was trying to explain."

"You lot get too easily over-excited, that's your trouble. You need to calm down a bit. Oh and Mike, your Mum and Dad were in touch. They can't wait to see you and your sister tomorrow. They're really busy trying to keep the department going while they look for another chief."

"So they're not letting the Professor back to the university then?" checked Mike.

"No – he's get the sack, I'm afraid," replied Uncle Charles. "Stealing rare bird's eggs is not a crime you can overlook. It's very serious stuff. The university can't possibly keep him in his job now."

*****

Tuesday

"Where are they?" said Sid the next morning as he looked round Holly's room. It was the day that Maggie, Mike, Emma and the twins were due to go home. Straight after breakfast all the children had dashed back upstairs.

"Look!" said Holly, pointing to the windowsill. In the middle of the row of dragons' eggs was a brand new egg shape, half red and half green.

"It's Sid and Colin's joined up key rings," said Emma.

"No, I've got my key-ring in my pocket," said Sid

"Me too," said Sid.

Maggie walked over to the shelf and touched the red and green egg shape. Two little bodies unfurled like a fern, then a little green head popped up, followed by a little red head. Both looked at her with blinking golden eyes then settled back down to sleep, making a perfect egg shape.

"Wow! How did Madam Verity know this would happen?" said Maggie, "She must have seen it in her crystal ball when she gave the twins those matching key rings!"

"At least we know they can safely disguise themselves as a key-ring if anyone comes in," said Mike.

"Are you sure they'll be okay?" asked Holly.

"They know how to look after one another," replied Maggie. "They've known for thousands of years."

Autumn stuck her nose out from under Maggie's bed.

"What have you got on your nose, Autumn?" Maggie said.

"She's got the two halves of the green egg shell off the window sill," said Mike. "Look! She's licked them clean."

Autumn wagged her tail. The green shell was shiny and clean like thick green crystal. Maggie picked up the two halves and put them safely in Holly's dressing table drawer.

"I hope it won't do her any harm," said Maggie, anxiously.

"Look!" said Sid. He was pointing at a tiny drop of golden dragon's egg yolk which had spilled onto the windowsill.

"It's like liquid gold!" said Colin. And before anyone could stop him, he had stuck two fingertips into it and then put one in his mouth and one in Sid's mouth.

"No!" said Maggie, but she was too late.

"Whatever did you do that for?" she shouted.

"I wasn't thinking…" said Colin.

"It's only magic egg yolk…" said Sid, pulling a face.

"You must never do that!" said Maggie.

"What does it taste like?" asked Mike, curious.

"A bit like blood," said Colin.

"Ugh!" said Emma.

Oh no, thought Maggie, *what have the twins done!* "We've got to see *Barglor* before we go home," she said out loud, "We don't know what we're supposed to do with the babies, how to look after them, if we have to feed them or anything."

"Holly and me have got about an hour before we have to be at school," said Dave, "so it's now or never."

"We don't know if the other dragons' eggs are going to start hatching either," said Mike.

Autumn, who had been feeling a bit strange since licking the dragon eggshell, started to scratch at the door to get out of the bedroom.

"Autumn looks a bit off-colour to me," said Emma.

"What's off- colour mean?" asked Colin.

"Not herself. A bit ill..." replied Maggie, "...it's what happens to people who stick their fingers into strange substances and put them in their mouths!"

"Let's take Autumn out quickly," said Mike, "Nanny and Rick have gone into the village to say goodbye to their friends.

"And Mum and Dad are busy getting ready to go to work," said Holly.

We're running out of time thought Maggie. *We're running out of time!*

"The other eggs haven't moved," she said, "but I suppose we had better start preparing for The Rising."

They collected all the dragons' eggs together and put them carefully in their rucksacks. They left the baby twin dragons till last as they looked so peaceful all curled around each other on the shelf.

"Shall we wake them or carry them as they are?" asked Emma, bending over them.

"As they are," said Maggie, "It'll be safer for them if they're asleep."

*****

The creature on the sea-bed opened its wet red eyes very wide. It squirmed furiously and bared its teeth. It began to scratch its claws angrily in the sand.

*****

When they reached the top of the mountain that was really a hill, Maggie said, "*Barglor* won't be about yet. It's not dark."

"Just knock on the rock!" shouted Sid, laughing, and Colin joined in chanting, "Knock on the rock! Knock on the rock!" and the twins danced round and round.

Autumn was watching the twins carefully. She walked over to the rock, made a strange growling noise and then gave a few short, sharp barks. The children were amazed to see the door in the rock slide open.

"Autumn just opened the doorway!" exclaimed Maggie. "She just spoke to it and it opened!"

They all gazed at Autumn with their mouths open. The dog took a few steps towards the doorway and looked straight at the children. She raised one paw as if signaling to them.

"Wow!" said Dave.

"Cool!" said Mike.

Barglor appeared at the tunnel entrance, looking rather flustered.

"The green egg hatched into two dragons, *Barglor*!" chattered Maggie eagerly.

"One green and one red," added Mike.

"Who was it who spoke to the dragons and opened the door?" *Barglor* asked. He was looking concerned.

"Autumn did!" said Maggie. "She just did it! I don't know how!"

"Maybe it's to do with eating some of the dragons' magic egg yolk," said Dave.

"Your dog ate the yolk?" asked *Barglor*.

"Yes," said Maggie. "She licked the shell clean. The twins tasted a drop too. Will it hurt them? Will the dragons be angry?"

"Are you feeling quite well?" said *Barglor.*

"Fine," said Sid.

"Me too," said Colin.

"Well, a small amount of the egg yolk should have very little effect," said *Barglor*. "Your dog, however, seems to have developed certain magical skills as a result. But she will come to no harm. Come quickly now. The dragons will wish to talk with you. We had better go to the Speaking Stone with no further delay."

He led the way through the tunnels, across the vast crystal cave and over to the Speaking Stone where the Stone Egg hummed loudly. As soon as the children rested their hands on the rock, the strange dragons' voices rumbled from within.

"Our trust in you has been well placed…" boomed the voices, "…two of our children have been safely born."

"I am very glad I was able to help," said Maggie, "but it's the Lava-Eaters you really need to thank."

A puff of smoke burst from around the Speaking Stone.

"We acknowledge our debt of gratitude to the Lava-Eaters," breathed the dragons, "although we do not speak to them and never will."

"Don't you think you've punished them enough?" asked Maggie. "I was wondering if you would consider letting them out."

She heard Mike draw his breath and hold it. Her finger nails dug into her palms as she clenched her fists. The other children stared at her in amazement. How brave of Maggie to speak to the powerful dragons in such a way!

"We thank you for your suggestion," growled the dragons. "We will consider it."

"The Lava-Eaters said there was another creature imprisoned somewhere," said Maggie, "or perhaps they meant you lot."

"We know of no other creatures," roared all the dragons.

"But you *must* know," insisted Maggie.

"We know of only two – the Lava-Eaters," rumbled the voices angrily.

"The dragons never lie," said *Barglor,* flapping his wings anxiously. "You must leave now!"

"Wait! Tell me what we need to do with your twin baby dragons?" asked Maggie. "We are going home today and won't be talking with you again!"

"They will sleep!" thundered the dragons, "until it is time. Do nothing but guard them well!" Then the vibration within the Speaking Stone died away.

"I'll show you out," said *Barglor*. Prepare to go to the Rising Place. Be on your guard. There is still much danger." *Barglor* flew from the Speaking Stone, hopped on to Autumn's back and whispered something in her ear. The dog turned her head and nodded. Clearly she was no longer just a dog with simple dog thoughts, but a dog with a purpose, a dog with a head full of images of times and places that she was sure she had never seen before. There were voices in her head too, and they spoke in a strange language that she was only just beginning to understand.

"Now listen, everyone," said Maggie in a very serious voice. "We're got to trust that The Rising is going to happen. We've got to get to the stones right now!"

"Over there!" yelled Mike suddenly. "Look! It's Madam Verity! She's come for The Rising!"

*****

"It's been years since I did this," said the old white dragon. "I wonder if I can still manage it." He stood up and opened his wings, stretching them wide like the sails on a ghostly ship. "Oooooohhhh!" he said. "That feels really rather good."

*****

They all climbed up the mountainside to the stone circle, Madam Verity leading the way.

Mike dumped Verity's bag on the ground.

"What on earth have you got in here?" he asked. "It weighs a ton!"

"I thought we ought to dress up for the occasion," Verity said as she unzipped the bag and handed round some bright, colourful clothes.

"I can't wear *this*!" said Dave, holding up a long orange velvet robe. They slowly realised that they were each holding a hooded robe of a different colour – colours that matched the seven eggs!

"They're like posh dressing gowns," said Emma.

"I love them!" said Holly.

"They're fabulous, Verity!" said Maggie, and put on her yellow one on, lifting the hood over her hair.

"It makes you look like a high priestess in a horror movie," said Mike, pulling on his blue one. "Oh, this is quite cool actually! Bit like Star Wars!"

"We look like a bunch of weirdo hippies," said Dave, still a bit reluctant.

"They're lovely and warm," said Holly, cuddling into her indigo robe.

"It didn't seem like a jeans and jumpers occasion," said Verity, lifting her own silvery grey hood and smiling as Colin and Sid pranced around in their red and green cloaks.

Then they all sat down on the grassy bank outside the stone circle. Maggie had placed the twin baby dragons down on the turf and Autumn was guarding them carefully. The children had placed their rucksacks containing the five un-hatched eggs in a pile next to Autumn - just to be on the safe side.

With a wild flapping of wings, *Keesoo* landed on top of Maggie's guardian stone. He removed his golden cloak and bowed low to Verity and the children. A dark cloud drew down over their heads and they heard the fluttering noise of many wings as bats and birds of every kind swooped down, becoming Egg Keepers and Dragon Speakers as they landed.

"The time has finally come," *Keesoo* announced. "We Egg Keepers thank you all for making this moment possible!"

"We Dragon Speakers too have much to thank you for," said *Barglor*, flying over to stand beside *Keesoo*.

"Thank you both!" said Maggie. "You know I'm very glad we could help. What happens now?"

"Remove the eggs you have brought with you and set them down on the ground," said *Barglor*. The children obeyed him.

"Wow…the ground's shaking!" marveled Dave.

Sure enough, the ground in the centre of the stone circle was swelling to form a small hill which then suddenly split in two, the grass curling back like the petals of a flower. Something was rising from the middle.

"The Cradle Stone!" gasped the children.

*****

The creature beneath the sea scratched with its claws, snorting great gushes of water from its flared nostrils. The red egg in its stomach burned like a hot coal. As it sought for the mind of the being it controlled, its tail whipped through the murky water, slicing it so deeply that huge waves formed on the surface. The creature ground its teeth together and made a screeching sound which shook the water from shore to shore.

*****

The Cradle Stone rose from the ground. The Stone Egg was balanced upon it, purring like a Persian cat on a velvet cushion. The world held its breath as the sun began to slide behind a vast black cloud and, although morning, it started to grow as dark as twilight. Rising through the grass in countless numbers, dragons' eggs of every possible colour caught the light of the disappearing sun, making the hillside blaze with rainbow firelight. A gentle breeze blew like a sigh and caressed the children's faces.

Then a triumphant cry tore through the air. Shocked, everyone turned to see Professor Falconer struggling over the brow of the hill! He stared around him madly, spotted them, and then came lurching and staggering straight towards them!

"What a shame," he snarled, "so many of your dear little eggs and so very pretty they all are, but I must destroy them all!"

Then his gaze fell upon the Stone Egg and he stopped in his tracks. "Ah-hah!" he cried, "The egg of eggs!"

And, from inside his jacket he pulled out a large hammer. He swung it around his head as he hobbled towards the Stone Egg, laughing wildly. "Get back all of you! I MUST DESTROY IT!!!"

Autumn stood up and rushed over to him, blocking his path and baring her teeth. She snarled like a lioness. Verity stood up and spread her arms out in front of the children to protect them.

"You must speak to him, Maggie," urged Verity. "You're the only one who can stop him."

"Please, Professor Falconer, leave us alone!"cried Maggie, bravely taking a step forward. "You must know how important this day is! Why do you want to destroy everything!?"

Professor Falconer paused, staggered, the hammer swinging awkwardly in his hands as he stared around him. The flocks of Egg Keepers and Dragon Speakers murmured and whispered under their breath. They looked terrified.

"The dark monster in my nightmares told me to destroy the eggs!" wailed the Professor. "He said that when I've destroyed them he will leave me alone. And I *want* him to leave me alone. I *want* to be left alone! I want to have a night's sleep without awful nightmares and terrible dreams! Don't you understand little girl?! I WANT TO BE LEFT ALONE!!!"

And raising the hammer high above his head, Professor Falconer staggered forward towards the Stone Egg. Autumn snarled at him from deep in her throat.

"Get him, Autumn!" shouted Maggie, not taking her eyes from Professor Falconer's face.

But just as the dog lunged at his legs to bring him down, Professor Falconer swung the hammer and accidentally caught poor Autumn a heavy blow on the side of her head. The children gasped in horror.

A crowd of Egg-Keepers put on their bird-cloaks and surged towards the Professor, covering his face with their flapping wings, while a crowd of Dragon-Keepers dive-bombed the top of his bald head. He staggered, fell backwards over a pile of rocks and banged his head on the ground where he lay there moaning and clutching his face.

Maggie ran over to Autumn and knelt beside her.

"Autumn!" shouted Maggie. "What have you done to my dog you horrible man!"

Maggie's tears fell onto Autumn's silent body as the other children stood frozen with horror. Mike and Dave took a step forward but Maggie held up her hand, gesturing to them to stay where they were.

"I think she's dead," she whispered. She reached out, stroking Autumn's side, staring at her in disbelief.

"Boys! Carry Autumn into the stone circle! Maggie, stand back! Quickly!" ordered Verity. "Put the dog near the Speaking Stone!"

With a struggle, Mike and Dave picked up Autumn's heavy limp body and staggered through the crowd of Egg Keepers and Dragon Speakers to the Stone Circle where they rested her next to the Speaking Stone.

"My darling dog…" Maggie said, burying her face in her fur. "Oh Autumn, please, please don't be dead!"

Then Emma shrieked, "Who's that?!

Two slow figures were lumbering across the field towards them.

Maggie turned. "It's the Lava-Eaters," she gasped, "They're free!"

"So many people…" murmured Adma gazing at them all.

"Hello, people…" said Deev.

"Hello," said Holly holding her hand out towards Deev, "Have you come to help Autumn?"

"Are you dragon-people?" said Sid.

"Do you really eat lava?" asked Colin.

But Maggie couldn't worry about the Lava-Eaters now. The Cradle Stone had started to rumble. Maggie put a protective arm around Autumn's body. She just couldn't stop crying. The rumbling grew louder and louder until it was deafening.

"We have released the Lava-Eaters!" rasped the dragons' voices from the depths of the Cradle Stone, "It is time for them to make amends!"

"We shall, for we know where the red egg is," said Deev.

"You do?" said Mike, staring at Deev.

"It is with the dark-minded creature," said Adma, "whose thoughts we hear but whose home is unknown to us."

The Cradle Stone shook as the voice roared out from it."How can this be?" it said. "You of all creatures have knowledge of the dragons and of the Earth and yet its home is unknown to you?"

"It guards its jealous mind," said Adma, "but we hear it as if through a fog. Its jealousy has separated it from all other creatures. It wants to stop The Rising."

"It wants the dragons to be angry with the Earth," said Deev, "because it wants the Earth for itself."

"And it has our red egg, you say?" rumbled the dragon voices. "Then we will send spies to track it down and reclaim it. We thank you. You are free to go."

"We are no longer human," said Deev, "We eat lava. What can we do with our lives if we remain above ground? We will be hunted down as curiosities. We will be captured and imprisoned once more."

"Eat fruit, much, much fruit," rasped the dragons. "Accept the marvellous gifts from the Earth. The fruits the earth offers so freely will heal you and soften your skin. You will soon look as human as the others."

Verity, pulling an apple from her picnic bag, handed it to Deev, who took it as if it were a precious treasure, bit into it, then passed it to Adma who ate some too. They chewed as if it was the most delicious taste they had ever experienced, their eyes shining with joy.

"Don't any of you see poor Autumn lying here!" cried Maggie to the others. "She's not breathing any more!"

"Put a piece of the apple inside the dog's mouth," rumbled the dragons. "She has eaten of the magic yolk so the powers of the dragons and the Earth will join up within her."

Adma bit away a piece of apple and pushed it between Autumn's lips. Every single hair on Autumn's body lifted a fraction of a millimetre. The Cradle Stone shook as Autumn tensed her body and gasped in a lungful of air, then another, and then another.

"Autumn!" shrieked Maggie.

Autumn lifted her head, twisted round towards Maggie and then jumped up to lick the tears from her face.

"Oh!" said Maggie, flinging her arms round Autumn. "Autumn, you've come back! You're not dead!"

With a joyous yap, Autumn bounded from one child to another, jumping up to lick them all.

"The Stone Egg is now ready," intoned the dragons. "The dragons' eggs are about to hatch. All of you take your places."

Keesoo stepped forward. The children and Verity moved around the sides of the circle where Egg Keepers and Dragon Speakers perched on every stone.

"The Egg Keepers wish to thank Maid Maggie and her six companions for making this special day possible," said *Keesoo*. "Maid Maggie was sent to us

214

because of The Legend. Helped by her loyal companions, she has protected the Stone Egg from many dangers."

The air rang with chirping and tweeting and cheering.

"Thank you," said Maggie, a little embarrassed.

Barglor flew to the Cradle Stone and cleared his throat.

"The Seven Guardians have also mended the rift between the Dragon Speakers and the Egg Keepers," said *Barglor*. "They have guarded our dragons' eggs and, when one was taken, Maid Maggie faced her worst fears to speak with the Lava-Eaters and save the situation. We owe them our thanks and our lives."

The Dragon Speakers cheered and clapped.

"Thank you once again," said Maggie. "We're all pleased we managed to help. I'm really very glad you're all speaking to each other again."

The humming from the Cradle Stone grew louder.

"We the Dragons, the Mountains of the Earth," intoned the dragons, "thank Maid Maggie, her brothers and her cousins who are the Seven of the Line. We have chosen them to guard the Seven who will remain. We also thank our sister Autumn for her heroism."

Autumn wagged her tail.

"Our own children, in answer to the Stone Egg's call, are now ready to rise with the Stone Egg," boomed the dragons. "Will the Seven of The Line now step forward to the Cradle Stone and present our eggs - our own precious children?"

The children felt overawed by the solemnity of the occasion, the strangeness of the setting. The colourful robes they wore made the situation feel even more unreal. Verity smiled at them and gently pushed them forward. The children rested the five rescued eggs on the Cradle Stone. Then the red and green twin dragons - who had been perching in the palm of Sid's hand - uncurled from each other and flew through the air to rest upon the Stone Egg.

There was a flash of brilliant white light and a series of loud explosions. The rescued dragons' eggs glowed like Christmas-tree lights before they each cracked open spilling a baby dragon onto the cradle stone. Each of the five baby dragons, after they had shaken themselves, sprayed drops of molten gold high into the air.

"A rainbow of dragons…" whispered Maggie.

The Stone Egg, pulsating like a beating heart, trembled, shimmered, and began to rise. The air had grown as dark as night. There was a loud cracking noise like a popcorn maker and the air was illuminated by the light of thousands and thousands of dragons' eggs hatching. The whole hillside became a sea of baby dragons and the air sparkled with gold dust. Like confetti swirling on the breeze, the dragon babies circled above the Stone Egg as it rose, the air rippling around them. The Stone Egg shone like the reflection of the moon on the sea, lighting the dark sky and rising upwards and upwards until the children, Verity and Autumn were leaning their heads back to see it. As the Stone Egg floated ever skywards, it seemed to develop a glistening silvery sheen.

"Look, the oceans are forming," whispered Verity to the children.

The Stone Egg continued its journey into the skies, climbing higher and higher, amid the clattering of thousands of baby dragons' wings as they flew up to curl around it.

"Hills and mountain ranges…" murmured Mike.

Then, with a roar of wings, all the Egg Keepers and Dragon Speakers flew up into the sky, darkening the air and obscuring the Stone Egg for a moment, but then it reappeared again, glowing like a star within a halo of birds and bats, high, high, high in the sky.

"It's almost gone!" exclaimed Maggie at last, when it was no more than a distant planet in a sky full of tiny stars. Night had come in day-time. It was like a miracle.

The seven children, Autumn, Verity and the Lava-Eaters stood on the hillside, gazing into the heavens.

"Look…" said Maggie, turning her head, "The Professor's gone!" They all turned to see and, sure enough, there was no sign of him.

"He's lost the battle," said Verity quietly. "He will not bother you any more. All of you will be left in peace."

"Where will The Stone Egg go?" asked Maggie.

"To form a new solar system," said Verity. "It will find a new sun and go into orbit around it."

"I shall miss our twin baby dragons," said Sid wistfully.

"Me too…" agreed Colin, with a bit of sniffle.

"Look at the Cradle Stone!" said Dave.

The dark air was disappearing in fog-like wisps and the sunlight was gradually returning. And there were the two red and green baby dragons along with five others! All seven baby dragons flew to land on the children's shoulders as the Cradle Stone sank slowly back into the ground. The grass closed over the magical place until the hillside was restored to its former state. The thousands and thousands of different coloured pieces of eggshell that littered the hillside began to crumble into sparkling dust which blew away on the gentle morning breeze.

Now a familiar black shape was coming towards them, blotting out the strengthening sun.

"And here comes *Keesoo*!" cried Holly.

"I've come to say my last goodbye," called *Keesoo*, as he landed beside the children. "And to tell you that if any of you Glorious Seven should ever need me, all you have to do is call me."

He bowed low and all the children bowed politely in return. "Thank you," said Maggie. "But what do we do with these baby dragons?"

Keesoo called to the baby dragons and all seven leapt from the children's shoulders and into the air.

"They'll do exactly as they please," said *Keesoo*, "don't worry about them. They will always stay near you, but will happily protect themselves. They know how to hide. They know how to survive. They have always known. Goodbye."

"It's all over then," said Maggie rather sadly as she waved goodbye. "We did it everyone! We actually saved the world!"

"That was absolutely amazing!" said Dave.

"Like the best movie ever!" said Mike.

"Or computer game!" said Colin.

"And we've still got *dragons*!" exclaimed Sid, putting her hand up to touch the tiny green dragon perched on his shoulder.

"Goodbye!" squeaked *Barglor*, suddenly landing on the grass at their feet.

"Goodbye, *Barglor*," said Maggie, "It's been great knowing you. Will we ever see you again?"

"Oh, I'll be around," said *Barglor*. "I always remember my friends. Watch out for me at dusk if you ever need my help. The sun is getting stronger by the minute and I should not be out in daylight! Goodbye!"

"Look…"said Verity, pointing to the Lava-Eaters who were outlined on the crest of the hill, their arms raised in salute. "There they go towards their new life…"

"Goodbye, Adma and Deev," said Maggie softly. "Take care."

*****

Beneath the deepest darkest sea, the creature screamed. It was a scream of such loneliness and desolation that fish stopped swimming, dolphins stopped playing, and sharks stopped eating their prey, but no-one on Earth heard it and there was nobody to care. Under the waves the creature could do nothing. It gazed at the red egg and howled. Caught up by a sudden swelling current, the red egg floated away from the creature's grasp. Somewhere deep inside itself, the lost, dark dragon knew it had failed once again.

*****

"Poor, lost dark dragon," said the old white dragon, gazing up at the sky. "I can hear the poor thing howling and screaming. I wish I could find a way to comfort it. Who can it possibly be, out there lost and all alone?" The old white dragon sighed. He gazed at the stars as, once more, he picked up his pen.

And he wrote:

The Visitor

On wings of hope he came. He flew unseen
Across the lonely wilderness of space.
By moonlight only can he show his face.
He bends no blade of grass where he has been,
Nor casts a shadow as he passes by.

220

He cannot find the company he seeks.
No creature understands the words he speaks,
But even though he weeps, his eyes are dry.
He writes in language no one understands,
Strange poetry that comes into his head.
And, in his nightmares, dreams of far-off
lands which make him tremble in his troubled
sleep.
He gazes at the moon and cries out loud.
The moon, uncaring, goes behind a cloud.
But the two beneath the ground are now above.
The last poem that arrives is sent with love.

The white dragon stopped writing. Despite the sadness in the poem, he felt strangely contented as if this was the last verse he was going to have to create for some time. He looked up from his book and saw something streak like a spark across the sky. "There it goes at last!" he shouted. "Good luck, brave little planet! Hurrah! Hurrah! Hurrah!" He stood holding his poetry book, staring in the direction that the shooting star had gone. Then he began to run, spreading his wings and taking off in the direction of the brand new world. "Wait for me!" he shouted. "Wait for me! I'm coming with you!"

*****

The sky was suddenly as bright as a laser show as a flash of April lightning lit up every detail of the landscape. A deep rumbling noise echoed around the mountains. Thunder claps rattled the children's hearts in their chests. Torrential rain fell like freezing needles and they all squealed out loud as they ran into the driveway of the house.

"Quick!" shouted Verity, over the noise of the storm. "Give me back the robes and then run inside before you all get soaked!"

Maggie turned to her, "Thank you, Verity," she said. "I couldn't have done this without you."

Verity smiled at her, "All we have to do is to be in the right place at the right time. Remember that always, my dear." And, as she picked up her bag and turned to go, the tiny dragons leapt into the air from the children's shoulders, flying round her head as if saying farewell. Then they soared up vertically and clung under the guttering, hanging like gargoyles around the edges of the roof.

"They'll look after themselves perfectly," said Verity, "just as *Keesoo* said."

*****

Maggie stood next to Nanny Gardner's car and watched as the others fussed around Rick's van with their rucksacks and bags. It was time for the long drive home. She was very quiet and very still. She was smiling to herself. *I did it*, she thought. *I actually saved the world*. There had been wonderful news waiting when they had ran into the warm, dry kitchen that morning. Her mother and father had a new baby girl, born at the very moment of The Rising. She was named Stella. It was another word for star. Maggie had never felt so happy in her entire life. There was a perfectly round day-light moon visible in the clear, deep blue morning sky and, arching high above the magical

mountain, was the biggest, brightest rainbow she had
ever seen.

*****

Full Moon. May Day.

A team of Morris dancers had taken their places on
the road. Their dark hats and socks were trimmed with
rainbow coloured ribbons. The small girl thought they
looked like crazy black crows as their dark frockcoats
flapped in the breeze. The crowd watched. The air
smelled of fried onions, candy-floss and popcorn.
Bubbles floated in the gentle air and a cloud of cherry
blossom petals fluttered down from a tree in the
cathedral garden onto the dancers in the street below.

"A dragon, Mum, look!" shouted the girl, tugging on
her mother's sleeve as she jumped up and down and
pointed at the shape that flapped towards the cathedral
spire.

"Yes, darling, some of the Morris dancers are
pretending to be a big dragon. He's quite scary isn't he?
He's going to fight a battle with St George, look!"

"This dance we are about to perform," announced one
of the Morris men, glaring at the eager crowd from
beneath his bushy eyebrows, "is from the Dark Side!"

"No, not the one that St George is going to fight!"
cried the small girl, "That's just pretend. This is a *real*
dragon – look!"

"It's just one of those helium balloons, darling," said
her mother, glancing up at the cathedral from the busy
street where the brightly dressed Morris dancers and
musicians were busy performing the battle. "It's going
to get caught up on the ledge. Would you like me to
buy you one?"

The sun was shining behind the cathedral spire. The girl screwed up her eyes as the small golden dragon landed on the stone ledge just below the cathedral roof, from where carved grey gargoyles grimaced down at the crowded streets. The little dragon clung fast to the ledge, struggling to get its balance. It seemed to be watching her. She stared at it as it gradually became motionless, its golden shades fading. In a few short minutes it had become the same drab colour as the gargoyles. It seemed to the small girl as if the dragon felt it had to hide.

"Mummy, the dragon is disappearing!" said the small girl.

"Is it, darling?" said her mother vaguely. "Then the battle must be over. Let's go home."

THE END.

Maggie's Family Tree

Holly	Dave	Maggie	Sid	Colin	Mike	Emma
10	12	11	9	9	12	8

Janie + Charles Edwards   Rose + Andrew Gardner   Lily + Stephen Harris

Nanny (Georgina) + Granddad Gardner   Granddad Greenwood
(who died some time ago)   (who lives in Australia)

Lightning Source UK Ltd.
Milton Keynes UK
UKHW031812090919
349469UK00002B/246/P